Urban Touch Entertainment
Presents

Summer's Distant Echoes

By James "I-God" Morris

James I-God Morris

Written by: James Morris for Urban Touch Entertainment
Published by: Urban Touch Entertainment
Editing/Typesetting by: Carla M. Dean,
U Can Mark My Word Editorial & Typesetting Services
Cover Design by: Marion Designs

ISBN: (13-digit) 97809771484-1-7
       (10-digit) 09771484-1-6

[1. Urban-Fiction 2. Drama-Fiction 3. Brooklyn-Fiction]

<u>Dedications</u>
This Book is dedicated to the mothers in my life

To My biological Mother Natalie Morris
You will forever live on in me. Through your womb I was facet, shaped, and molded in the image and likeness of Divinity.

To my aunt Poopie (Gwendolyn Morris)
You raised me, and I am who I am because of your compassion and drive.

To my Grandmother Henry
When all I wanted was the street and the streets had no love, you and Granddad were my Rock.

To my grandmothers Winnie Parker and Grace
Words cannot express how grateful and lucky I was to have the two of you. The both of you will love forever in my memories and heart.

To the Mothers of my children
Through your wombs I will live forever.

Acknowledgements

Throughout life travels there are many obstacles to defer you from the straight and narrow path. Acknowledgement is best given through your actions and not words. For the people who have touched my life, which are so few, my acknowledgements are greater than words, greater than placing names on this page. My acknowledgements are seen through my compassion and drive to pass on the jewels and blessings of life to others.

To the Father Allah, Justice, the firstborns and the first fruits of the nation of Gods and Earths, thank you for bestowing the breath of life and breathing into my nostrils the science and culture of I-God. Through Truth I was born alive.

To my old dad, Big Mo (James Morris), thank you for life. More and more each day, I see how you and I are the same. I-See Allah, hold your head good. Your book is next lil' bro. To my numerous cousins, aunts, uncles, nieces, and nephews, I got y'all back.

Special acknowledgements are due to my Earth Queen, I-Mecca Earth, and my Urban Touch Entertainment family. Thank you for having the patience. Patience is truly a virtue.

To my Amiaya family, Inch (it won't be long now, son) and Tonia, thank you for the support.

To my children, through y'all I remain eternal: Dequan I-God, Quatasia Shah Queen, Divine I-Asiatic, Bismi Allah, He-Allah Supreme, My-Queen Medina, Eternal I-God and I-Paradise.

To my readers, what good is my work without you?
To all the street vendors, bulletproof Love.

To C&B Books, Caroline Rogers and Brenda Piper, thank you for everything.

Summer's Distant Echoes

By

James "I-God" Morris

Summer of 1997…

"Yo, son, what's your problem?"

"What? Who the fuck you think you talking to?"

"I'm saying, you see me with my lady, and you're being real disrespectful by staring at her ass like I'm not standing here."

"Hold up, nigga. I can stare at whatever I want. You shouldn't have your bitch out here dressed like that anyway. I'ma look, and if you turn your head, I'ma try it."

"What? Nigga, you tryin' to play me?!"

"Be-Real, please, just come on…let's go." Aware of Be-Real's blinding jealousy, Lyric pulled on his arm as she pleaded with him not to get into an altercation. So enraged, he didn't even notice the dude he was beefing with had a crew, who were standing against a nearby wall and wearing red bandanas. Within seconds, they moved and surrounded Be-Real.

Lately, Brooklyn had become the stomping grounds for gangs. The streets were becoming a war zone for the Bloods and Crips. At one time, it was said that gang shit would never make it to New York, but today, New York was more like Cali, with its colors and the thugs who would die for them.

Lyric pulled Be-Real away from the crowd that started forming. "Come on, daddy. It's not worth it. We have two beautiful girls to go home to." Lyric reminded Be-Real of their two daughters who were eleven months apart, Summer being nine years of age and Destiny eight. Be-Real and Lyric had been together since they were sixteen years old, and had their first daughter at the age of seventeen. Knowing Be-Real loved his two angels more than anything in the world, she knew that once she mentioned them he would calm down and think about his actions.

Be-Real had just come home from federal prison for credit card fraud. He had stolen a total of 250G's, and with the money, had invested in real estate, being smart enough to put the property in Lyric's name. Lyric, one of the hottest new R&B singers out, had just signed a record contract, which was the reason why her and Be-Real were out celebrating.

"Yeah, bitch-ass nigga, you better listen to your bitch and keep it moving if you know what's good for you!" The dude jumped up in Be-Real's face just as Lyric pulled him away. "Yeah, your best bet is to go home with that big butt girl of yours before you get both of y'all asses touched up something special."

"A'ight, Duke, you got it. I'ma see you again," Be-Real responded as Lyric pulled him out of the club. It took everything Be-Real had not to punish the dude, who knew he was at a disadvantage because he had Lyric with him. However, as soon as he dropped her off at home, he planned on making a round-trip to get at this nigga for disrespecting him. Be-Real wasn't no pussy, and he couldn't have no pussy nigga trying to play him, either. Be-Real knew the dude from someplace, but couldn't place his finger on where. As for the dudes with him, they couldn't have been any older than sixteen. They shouldn't have even been in the club, but this was Brooklyn and who gave a fuck nowadays?

When they stepped outside the club, it was slightly drizzling, the rain cooling the summer's heat. Be-Real used his throwback jersey to cover Lyric's hair as they both ran to the S500 Benz they just purchased. As he opened the passenger side door for Lyric, he heard the sound of feet running towards them. Be-Real hurried Lyric into the car and spun around. Just then, the dude from the club and four other men surrounded him.

"Yo, muthafucka, what's all that shit about you gonna see a nigga? You threatenin' a nigga?" All five men quickly drew their guns.

"Hold up, man. I don't want any problems. Me and my girl are just trying to go home, that's all." Be-Real could hear Lyric screaming as he tried to keep his cool and not panic. Even though he knew he was in a fucked-up predicament, his main concern was Lyric. Be-Real looked into the eyes of the dude he had words with in the club, and then in the faces of the four men. He could tell they were itching to shoot him, if for nothing more than to get a rep. Then it hit him! He knew where he recognized the dude from. He was a nobody that became a Blood while in prison because the Latin Kings had him under pressure, and shortly after, Be-Real had a beef with him over turning the TV channel in the dayroom.

Before Be-Real could say anything, one of the lil' shorties snatched his Cuban link with the iced-out moneybag pendant. Off of reflex, Be-Real rushed the shorty, but was stopped in his tracks by a deafening sound followed by a sharp pain in his chest. As Be-Real fell to the ground, he heard a series of shots, and then he no longer heard Lyric's screams.

Be-Real's final thought was of Lyric.

Chapter 1:
Summer's Big Night

"Summer, come on! Your date is here!" Destiny screamed from the bottom of the steps up to Summer, who was upstairs getting ready for the prom. "That girl's been in her room since five o'clock. She must really be trying to impress your butt, Brian. Do you want something to drink while you wait? You might be here another thirty minutes. You know how Summer gets."

Not awaiting a response, Destiny disappeared into the kitchen to get Brian a glass of lemonade.

Brian and Summer had been dating since the eighth grade and planned to take their relationship a step further tonight after the prom. They had planned this day all year. This was their biggest moment, the end of school. Decked out in Armani from head to toe, Brian also had on the burgundy gator shoes Summer had picked out to match his burgundy gator belt. He had spent well over eight thousand dollars on his outfit.

Brian, the star point guard for his basketball team, planned on going to the pros straight from high school, which was against everybody's better judgment. Brian had a pro game, but his reading and math were below grade average. The only reason he made it through school was due to his coach and his ability to take his high school to the state championship every year.

"Hey, Brian, you look real cute in your suit," Ms. Hardy complimented while exiting the kitchen. "You should dress like that more often. I can't stand when you men wear y'all pants hanging all off their ass as if they have no home training. I love to see a man in some nice slacks and a decent dress shirt." Ms. Hardy, Lyric's mother, was Destiny and Summer's grandmother. She took the girls in when their parents were murdered.

"Thank you, Ms. Hardy. I see where the girls get their beauty from." Brian handed her a bouquet of flowers he was holding.

"Who are these for?"

"They're for you, a token of my appreciation."

"Awww, that's so sweet, baby. Let me see what's keeping this girl so damn long." Ms. Hardy walked out of the living room to go upstairs.

At the same time, Destiny came out of the kitchen with the lemonade. Destiny and Summer, who were both the spitting image of their mother, could have passed for twins since they were so close in age, except Destiny was darker in complexion like her father.

"Here, Brian. Summer didn't bring her slow ass down them damn stairs yet?" Destiny passed Brian the glass as she picked up the phone to page her man who was supposed to have arrived an hour ago. "Summer, hurry your butt up!" Destiny shouted while dialing the number.

"Your grandmother just went upstairs to get her. Yo, Destiny, you know my man Short Dog is trying to get with you. He told me to holla at you for him."

"Brian, please," she laughed, "you know a nigga got to have long paper to get with this. I'm not like my sister. I need a man that can support my every financial need. Short Dog, with his nickel and dime crack-selling ass, can't do anything for me." She laughed again before continuing. "What? He wants to buy me some sneakers. Come on. I'm not a chicken-head broad. Tell 'em if he wants to get with this, he got to be willing to take a sistah on shopping sprees and load me with diamonds. You can't get this with any package money. A nigga has to push weight. Plus, Shorty is a little too young for my taste."

"Come on, Destiny, he is the same age as you. Your ass ain't nothing but sixteen."

"Yeah, but we mature quicker than y'all do."

Brian sipped from the glass as he admired how sexy Destiny was. If he weren't with Summer, he would have definitely tried to get at Destiny. They both were fine as hell. Nevertheless, Destiny was a little wilder and loose. Summer was still a virgin, but Destiny had already had two abortions and the crowd she hung out with was wild, smoked trees, partied, and stayed in some type of drama. Her and Summer were complete opposites, like night and day.

"Plus, Brian, you know I fuck with Rashawn now."

"Girl, please, the only reason you're with that ugly nigga is because he has the block on lock. But your ass better be careful 'cuz I hear them niggas on Gates is gunning for that nigga. Many cats hate on son." Brian paused to take a sip on his drink. "I heard them niggas hit his Range up. So be careful when you are riding around with that nigga. You know money is the root to all evil, and I don't want you getting caught up in that nigga's shit."

"I feel you, but don't worry about me. What you need to be worrying about is my slow-ass sistah. Y'all better not do nothing I wouldn't do." Destiny smiled. "As a matter of fact, I wish you *would* because she needs some dick so she can loosen up. She's been too uptight lately. I told her that she needs some dick. That shit should get her right so she can live a little. So make sure you do all of us a favor and tap that ass."

"Destiny, you're crazy."

They both laughed.

BEEP...BEEP...BEEP...

Destiny ran to the window. Outside, an all-black Escalade trimmed in chrome and banging 50 Cent's "Candy Shop" waited for her.

"I'm coming!" Destiny yelled out the window. "Well, Brian, that's my cue. You and my sistah have a good time. Don't keep her out all night, either." Destiny nudged Brian in the side. "A'ight, Ma, I'm gone," Destiny hollered upstairs as she left the house without waiting for a response. "Ma" is what they called their grandmother.

About fifteen minutes later, Summer descended the stairs dressed in a burgundy satin, curve-hugging Dolce & Gabbana gown. Stunned by her beauty, Brian's mouth damn near dropped to the floor. Summer was drop-dead beautiful and she knew it. "Damn, Summer! You know you're going to turn heads tonight." Brian approached Summer, kissed her on the cheek, then grabbed her by the hand and led her outside to his brand-new Benz truck, which was a graduation present from his agent. Ms. Hardy followed close behind them.

"Now, Brian, treat my baby like a woman tonight and take good care of her. I'm holding you responsible for her well-being. If one hair is out of place, your ass is mine," Ms. Hardy joked as she gave Summer a hug and kiss. "Girl, if Brian doesn't act right, don't hesitate to call. I'll be right there regardless of the time."

"Alright, Ma, you're embarrassing me." Summer hurried and jumped in the truck. "Brian, whose truck is this?" she asked after he sat behind the wheel. Summer looked around the interior of the Benz, admiring the TVs and navigation system.

"It's mine. Do you like it?"

"Oh boy! Look at you! I know you really gassed up now." Summer smiled as she turned on the music and Brian pulled off.

"Nah, this is just a little something something from my agent to show me what's in store for me. It's a good look for me, right?"

"Shiiit! It's a hell of a look, and I make it look just that much better." Summer reclined the seats as she thought about the events they had planned for tonight.

Summer was still a virgin, but after tonight, she planned on entering womanhood. She and Brian had been together for years, and he never pressured her to do nothing she didn't want to. In fact, she got more pressure from her sister for being a virgin than she did Brian. Destiny started having sex when she was fourteen, but Summer chose to wait until she graduated from high school, which is probably why she graduated with honors. Ever since their parents were killed, Summer and Destiny took on two very different personalities. Summer was into school and kept to herself, while Destiny became fascinated with the streets and continued to fail in school. Destiny was hype and wild like their father, whereas Summer was more ladylike and family oriented like their mother.

"Summer, I have something for you. Look in the glove compartment; there's a box for you." Before Brian could finish what he was saying, Summer was in the glove compartment.

"Brian, what is it?"

"Open it and find out."

Summer tore into the neatly wrapped box. "Oh! Brian, it's beautiful." Summer held up the diamond bracelet, leaned over, and gave him a kiss. "Thank you. I love it."

"Don't worry…you'll have plenty of time to thank me later." Brian smiled as he continued driving to their destination.

* * * * *

"Yo, Rashawn, I think we should move on them cats from the new side. Lately, they've been getting real fly out the mouth. The heads been complaining about those niggas threatening them about copping from us and not them. Ms. Sadie just told me that lil' nigga Ski pulled a gun on her and told her if she didn't start copping from them that he would bust a cap in her ass. He got her scared to death to cop. She also told me that they have been stepping to all of our customers." Spyda pulled on Rashawn's headrest as he leaned forward from the backseat to pass Rashawn the blunt.

"Nigga, what I tell you about pulling on my muthafuckin' headrest?" Rashawn barked as he motioned for Destiny to take the blunt from Spyda.

Spyda was one of Rashawn's top "yes men". They both grew up in Smurf Village, a housing project for low-income families. When he was younger, Rashawn was hit by a bus, and his mother sued the bus company and settled for 250 thousand dollars. After turning eighteen, he got his first piece of money, which he used to purchase a big fancy car, jewelry, and some weight. Him, Spyda, and their lil' man Smooth have been flipping weight ever since. About a year ago, though, Smooth was killed in a beef they had with some Jamaicans who tried to move on a block they were hustling. Rashawn and his crew have been banging hard ever since they got on and have been through numerous wars. They have established themselves as a force to be recognized in the hood.

Rashawn ignored Spyda's comment about the cats from the new side. Smurf Village was broken up in two parts, the old side and the new side. The new side was called this because a couple of years ago contractors started fixing the projects up with new windows, doors, and by cleaning the buildings. The run-down buildings started to look halfway decent, but they lost the contract and wasn't able to finish the remaining units. However, compared to the unfinished side of the project, the side completed looked brand new.

On the new side, a cat named Butter Bean and his crew of youngbloods was on the come-up making a lot of noise. They were gunning for what Rashawn and Spyda had built in the project. Butter Bean was a short, dark-skinned cat with 360 waves in his hair and a cut on the side of his face that he got upstate while on the phone. Butter Bean had only been home a couple of months after serving a three to nine year bid for robbery, and already they've been in numerous confrontations. Now, Butter had his eyes on what Rashawn had.

While growing up, Butter Bean went to the same school as Rashawn and Spyda, although he was a couple of years older than they were. But in this game, it didn't matter how long you knew a person; your brother became your enemy when money, power, and respect were involved. Just because you grew up in the same projects or went to the same school that held no weight. How much you were willing to hold on to, and what you were willing to do to hold on to it, is what counted. The majority of the wars Rashawn and Spyda had were with dudes they knew or grew up with. That's just the way things were when you lived in a housing complex and everybody wanted to escape the reality of poverty with their eyes on the American dream. The only way it seemed for the young cats in these housing complexes to achieve these dreams was through the cut-throat life of the streets. Living in these conditions made a boy's heart cold, so when they grew into manhood, they were conditioned to love and trust no one. The only God to most of these lost souls in these concentration camps was the code of 'DA GAME'.

The only thing Rashawn somewhat cared about was his son, Jamal, who was nine years old and lived with his grandmother. Jamal's mother, Sha, was in prison for conspiracy and due out within a month. She had taken the weight for some drugs found in Rashawn's car over six years ago.

Rashawn found himself in a difficult situation because he had grown closer to Destiny, but knew he couldn't have her around when Sha came home. Although young, Destiny is what Rashawn wanted in a shorty, one who would go all out for her man. Destiny reminded Rashawn of Sha so much. She carried herself in the same manner and they were both short and dark skin. Rashawn didn't want to let Destiny go, but he knew Sha wouldn't go for him fucking with Destiny after she had done all those years for him. Sha felt Rashawn owed her. However, something about Destiny made it hard for Rashawn to let go. Besides being thick as hell and one of the prettiest things around, she was a soldier that would bust her gun without hesitation. She was all of this at the age of sixteen, so Rashawn could actually visualize what a few years under his wing would do for her.

Rashawn's thoughts were broke by Destiny rubbing on his leg. "Rashawn, where are we going?" she asked as she passed him the blunt after puffing on it.

"We going to drop Spyda off at the Pj's, and then I want you to make a run with me to this bitch Charlene's house. I need you to put some fear in her. She owes me a couple of hundred when she gets her back pay from SSI this month. I just need you to smack her up a lil'. After that, we're going to the hotel so I can take care of that wet, sweet thang that's been waiting for my touch all night. Would you like that?"

"Mmmm, Daddy, you know how to make a girl feel good." Destiny rubbed on Rashawn's thigh as he navigated through traffic.

"Ayo, Destiny!" Spyda called out, breaking the mood Rashawn and Destiny were in.

"What's up, Spyda?" she answered in an irritated tone.

"Why you never hook a brother up with that fine ass sistah of yours? I'm feeling Summer," Spyda said as he once again pulled on Rashawn's headrest to lean forward. Rashawn just shook his head, trying not to get annoyed by Spyda pulling on his headrest.

"Spyda you know my sistah don't like fucking with no thugs. Besides, she has a boyfriend."

"That's right…she's going out with that lil' nigga that plays ball. I heard he's supposed to be going to the NBA next year."

"Yeah, Brian is a good guy, and he gives my sistah whatever she wants."

"Yeah, that lil' nigga eating well off that basketball shit, too. I saw him earlier today pushing a brand-new Benz SUV." Spyda sat back in his seat as he unfolded a ten dollar bill filled with cocaine, and started sniffing. "So Rah, what's the happs with making that move to Ohio with Justice?"

"Son, I don't know. I don't even like that lil' nigga. It's something about his sneaky ass that makes me not like the nigga. Maybe because every time I turn around he's getting locked up and always gets right the fuck out. I don't trust that type of shit."

"What if we send them niggas Chuck and Hunt with him? You know they'll keep a good eye on that nigga. Plus, you know the money will be legit."

"Yeah, that's okay, but I don't want the nigga knowing I have anything to do with that shit because I don't trust him. But if you want to do that, it's on you and he's your responsibility." Rashawn pulled up in front of the Pj's and Spyda gave him a pound before getting out. "Yo, I'ma holla at you later."

"A'ight, Rashawn, hit me later. One!"

"Destiny, I have something for you. Look in the glove department," Rashawn said after pulling off. Destiny went into the glove department and pulled out the only thing in there. It was a Ziploc bag containing about an ounce of fish scale cocaine.

"Rashawn, what's this?" Destiny asked, already knowing the answer. Nevertheless, she tried to figure out why Rashawn said he had something for her as she studied the contents of the bag.

"Come on, Destiny, you know what that is. It's '*GIRL*' cocaine. Tonight, I want you to get high with me. I want you on the same plane I'm on."

"Rashawn, you know I don't mess with no hardcore drugs. Strictly weed and getting my drink on."

"Come on, Boo." Rashawn took the bag from her. "This is for the grown and sexy. We're on a different scale; it's time for us to step our game up. You're not hanging with your lil' girlfriends no more. We on some big money shit. Are you with me or what?"

"You know you don't even have to ask me that. I'll do anything for you."

"So go ahead and hit that. Take a taste. I bet you'll never turn back. Moreover, it makes the sex super. Have you ever had multiple orgasms? If not, the magic in this bag will do the trick."

Rashawn passed the bag back to Destiny, who took a sniff. Not knowing what to do, she put her nose in the bag and inhaled, taking cocaine up both nostrils. She froze momentarily as her whole face went numb. Destiny found herself in a comatose-like state, hearing nothing but Rashawn's laughter. It seemed as if everything had slowed down but she was moving at super speed. After the initial feeling passed, Destiny felt alive and carefree. Rashawn's words became clear to her, and she could make out what he was saying.

"Damn, girl, you got to take it easy. You can't just jump in there and try to sniff the whole bag at once." He continued laughing.

Being young and naïve, Destiny was willing to do whatever Rashawn wanted her to do just to be accepted by him. She enjoyed the immediate gratification she got from the cocaine and continued sniffing as Rashawn drove.

"This shit got my heart beating fast! Is that supposed to happen?" Destiny asked as she sniffed the cocaine up each nostril, one at a time.

"Yeah, don't worry about that. That just mean it's in your system. Do you like it?" Destiny shook her head as she continued to indulge. "I told you, you'd like it."

After about twenty minutes, Rashawn pulled up to an old apartment building. He reached under the seat and passed Destiny the .357 auto he had stashed. Destiny asked no questions as Rashawn got out. She simply tucked the gun in her bag, got out, and followed Rashawn.

* * * * *

"Yo, Butter Bean, them cats on the old side is eating real well and the Bloods are struggling. That nigga Rashawn is trying to monopolize the game. He got them niggas pushing crack, cocaine, and weed. He's even trying to get them to rent out the center to them every Friday and Saturday night so he can throw parties with strippers. Something got to give."

"You know what, Scooby, those fools don't think it can happen." Black Supreme passed Bloody Dog the bottle of knotty head they were downing.

"Yo Blood, Rashawn and those niggas on the old side is kinda strong and they're deep out there." Black Supreme turned the bottle up.

Butter Bean looked at the three of his lieutenants and shook his head. He couldn't believe what he was hearing. Butter took a drag from his Newport before speaking.

"Yo Dogs, what that Blood be like?" he asked in a raspy voice.

"Murder all day!" they answered simultaneously.

"A'ight then, that's what the fuck I'm talking about. I have three older brothers that are serving life in the pen for a double homicide of a nigga and his bitch eight years ago who tried to play the Blood set. They ain't ever coming home, and they're still putting in work to show what that red be like. Them lil' niggas on the old side don't pump the substance that sustains life. We are that Blood force; we are the Mighty Blood nation. When the dogs bark, there's a vicious bite that comes with that. So y'all niggas man the fuck up! If we got to, we'll drop them niggas one by one." Butter Bean pulled out a bag of Crazy Eddie and threw it on the table in front of the three men. "Roll this shit so I can get dusted, then go paint the old side of the Pj's red. Y'all know what that red be like."

* * * * *

When Brian and Summer pulled up to the club, there was all type of limos parked in front.

"Damn, it looks like everybody decided to come in a limo tonight," Summer commented as Brian exited the truck and walked around to open the door for her. "Awww, ain't that so sweet. My prince charming." Summer took Brian's hand, as she stepped out of the truck.

"You better enjoy it now, because after I hit the draws, all this Mr. Charming shit is out the door." Brian flashed a devilish grin.

"Boy, you better stop playing before you don't get nothing but a cold shower tonight." Summer shoved Brian in the forehead with her finger.

"Baby girl, you know I'm just playing."

"You better be. Are you ready for a good time tonight?"

Brian grabbed her by the hands and kissed them. "You just don't know. I've been waiting for this night since

I started high school. Come on; let's show these people how to celebrate the beginning of our adulthood."

As they walked to the club, they could feel all eyes on them. They were both laced with diamonds and dressed to impress. They could feel the hatred in the air when they walked by a group of people standing outside the entrance waiting to get in, but they didn't have any invites. Nearby, a group of juniors stood around to see who was wearing and driving what so they could have something to talk about in school the next day. As soon as they entered the club, Summer heard a familiar voice calling her name.

"Summer!"

Brian and Summer both spun around to find Cookie and Penny coming their way. Cookie and Penny, being first cousins, were also graduating this year. Summer, Cookie, and Penny attended the same church and sung in the church's choir. Cookie's mother and lil' sister had moved to Virginia last summer, but Cookie stayed behind with Penny and her mother so she could finish school. Cookie's mother, Ms. Diana, was battered by Cookie's father for years before she finally got up the courage to leave him.

"Hey, girl! Y'all looking real cute together," Penny said while giving Summer and Brian a kiss on their cheeks.

"What's up, y'all? Who are the lucky men who got trapped with y'all tonight? Or should I say the *unlucky* men?" Summer asked as she hugged Cookie.

"Girl, you know ain't nobody trying to put up with Penny's picky ass. So, I had to accompany her."

"Hey, y'all, they spiked the punch; come on." Penny pulled Summer and Cookie by the arms, leaving Brian standing there by himself like he was lost.

* * * * *

Outside the club, and off to the side sitting in the dark scheming and hating, was a crew of stick-up kids looking for their next victims.

"Yo, Cy, wasn't that that nigga Brian?"

"Yeah, that's that nigga. He's shinning real good."

"That nigga getting that NBA money. I heard he got a three million dollar contract with Adidas. I know he got some cream on him. "

"Fuck the money! Between the both of them, they have on enough ice for us to go cop one of them things from Rashawn, plus pay him the money we owe him." Cy turned to his lil' man and passed him the 9mm. "When they come out, get 'em."

Chapter 2
A Difference from Night and Day

Boom...Boom...Boom...

"Who in the fuck is banging on my damn door like that?" Charlene snatched her door open without bothering to look out the peephole. Since she kept a steady flow of traffic from the baseheads who needed a place to get high, she figured it to be one of her "get high" buddies. As soon as she opened the door, she was staring down the barrel of a gun in the hands of a girl she didn't know. Charlene slowly backed away from the door as Destiny entered with the gun pointed at her head. When Charlene's eight-year-old saw the gun, she started screaming and ran to the back of the house.

"What the hell is going on? Who are you?" Charlene asked while trying not to panic. She looked into the eyes of the girl holding the gun, which was just as big as she was, and tried to figure out what had she done to this person for her to be up in her house pointing a gun in her face. *"Did I trick with this girl's father and her mother found out? Or did I rob the girl's man for a package?"* Charlene thought silently to herself.

She had done so much dirt she didn't know what to think. Then everything came to a head when Rashawn walked into the house. "Rashawn! What the hell is going on? Tell this lil' bitch to get this gun out of my face! How you gonna have somebody come up in my house and disrespect me and my kids?" Charlene tried to walk towards Rashawn.

CRACK!

Charlene fell to the floor, clutching the side of her face.

"Bitch, don't move! What? You think this shit is a game?" Destiny liked the feeling of power she had when holding the gun in her hands. It was an overwhelming feeling to create such fear in a person. Not to mention, the cocaine made her feel as if she was invincible. "Now listen, you owe my man a lot of money, and everyday the shit gains interest. Therefore, here's what's going to happen. We're going to send somebody here tomorrow with a package, and we want you to help them move the work. This is going to go on until you get your SSI check, and at the same time, you can make some money for yourself instead of digging yourself in deeper debt. Do you understand?" When Charlene didn't respond fast enough, Destiny hit her across the face with the gun once again, knocking her back down to the floor.

CRACK!

"Bitch, I asked you a question! Now, do you understand?"

"Yes," Charlene whispered in a faint voice while looking from Destiny to Rashawn. She couldn't believe he was doing this to her. She had known Rashawn since he was a baby, and even babysat him for his mother when she worked late and didn't have a babysitter. Not to mention, Charlene was the first girl to give him some head when he was thirteen years old. Charlene was only a couple of years older than Rashawn, and her older sister and Rashawn's mother were the best of friends; they practically grew up together. Now, he stood in her house allowing a girl she knew from nowhere to pistol whip her while he watched.

Impressed by her work, Rashawn looked at Destiny and smiled. "Come on, killer, that's enough." Rashawn pulled Destiny as he turned and left Charlene's house. As they walked to the car, Rashawn threw Destiny the keys. "Here, you drive." They both got in the car, and Rashawn reached into the glove department and took out the package.

"Daddy, how did I do?" Destiny asked, hoping she had pleased Rashawn.

After taking a sniff, Rashawn sat back and let the cocaine work through his system before answering Destiny's question. "You did real good, Boo, but what made you think of having her work off her debt to me in her crib? You can't give no fiend work to hustle."

"I know that, Daddy. That's why I told her that you would send somebody to work her house. Anyone can tell she keeps a lot of crackhead friends over. Her house has the potential to be a gold mine, and at the same time, she can make some money and pay off her debt. If you give her that chance, she'll be loyal to you, and as long as I keep that fear in her, she'll respect you. So, instead of you doing harm to her, you're giving her the opportunity to do for herself and her kids. Besides, the Pj's is getting hot; it's summertime and shit be off the hook. So you're going to need a change of location."

Feeling on top, Destiny navigated the Escalade through the Brooklyn streets with confidence. Impressed with the way Destiny spoke, and feeling her gangsta attitude, Rashawn had a sudden desire to fuck this young thug.

"You know what, Destiny? You have a strong business mind and that's what I need, somebody to take charge and make a difference. How in the hell a pretty girl like you become so street?"

"They say I'm just like my father," she answered. "I guess the fruit don't fall too far from the tree. My father was a hustler, and I guess I'm the inheritor of that trait." Destiny smiled. "Where to, Daddy?"

"Drive to my crib so I can take special care of my lil' thug. Like they say, thugs need love, too."

* * * * *

By midnight, the prom was on blast and everybody was drunk or damn near it. The spiked punch did its job. Brian and Summer were on the dance floor all night enjoying each other's company. The punch had them both feeling real horny and ready to explore what they had been planning for this night. When Omarion's "O" came on, everybody started coupling up and slow grinding.

"Summer, I want to be with you for the rest of my life. Having you in my arms sends chills through my entire body, and I never want this feeling to end. You are the one for me. I leave for training camp next week with the Miami Heat, but I'll send for you the following week."

Brian grabbed Summer and held her tight as he sucked on her neck. Summer could feel Brian's manhood rising, which in turn aroused her. His touch made her virgin walls pulsate and she enjoyed the feeling. Having mixed feelings, she was both afraid and anxious. She wanted to please Brian and felt it was time to give herself to him, but at the same time, she was afraid of the pain. All her friends told her the first time would hurt. Yet, she was ready; tonight was the night.

"Brian, I'm ready to leave. Let's go so we can be alone," Summer whispered in his ear as she laid her head on his shoulders while they grinded their hips to the music.

On their way out, Summer pulled Penny off the dance floor and told her to let Cookie know her and Brian were leaving.

Penny looked at Summer and Brian before screaming, "Ooooo, y'all going to do the nasty! It's about time your dick-teasing ass gave that thang up. That's right, Brian, make sure you handle my girl right."

Penny and Summer looked at each other and in unison said "*Okay!*"

"No, but seriously, y'all are made for each other." Penny then whispered in Summer's ear, "It's about damn time. You bet not let this good man slip out of your hands. Not to mention, girl, he's going to rub elbows with Shaq, and have money out his ass." Penny gave Summer a hug like it would be her last time seeing her.

"Alright, sis, I'll see you tomorrow."

As they departed the prom, they staggered and laughed while holding each other in their arms. The same people who were standing out front when they arrived were staring at them. Brian helped Summer into the truck. As he closed the door behind her, he noticed the crew staring and pointing at him. He could tell from their body language that they were scheming. He hurried and got in his truck, paying them no mind once he pulled off.

* * * * *

After Summer and Brian left, Penny walked to the phones in the hallway.

"Hello, Capone? Yeah, I'm 'bout to leave. Everybody knows I was here, so that's my alibi. I'm on my way now."

* * * * *

Spyda and a couple of his homies were out in front of their building conducting business as usual. The workers were handling all the hand-to-hand combat while Spyda was telling Chuck and Hunt about the Ohio move with Justice and Magnum. While they were talking, a short light-skinned mommy, who could pass for Spanish, walked towards them. She wobbled as her stomach looked as if she was in her last trimester of her pregnancy.

"Oh shit, Dog, don't look now, but here comes your over-pregnant baby mama," Hunt said before he and Chuck spun off and walked over to where the workers were serving a fiend. Spyda and Linda had a four-year-old son together and expecting their second baby any day now.

"Damn!" Spyda mumbled to himself as Linda fast approached. He braced himself for the ear beating he knew was coming because he had ignored her pages all day.

"Spyda, why the hell haven't you called me back? I've been calling and paging you all day. You could have at least called. Your ass didn't care if I went into labor to have this damn baby or not. You're out here with these no-good ass niggas all day, but when your ass wants some pussy or your sour dick sucked, you all up in my face." Linda pointed her finger in Spyda's face.

"Damn, girl, why you out here acting like that? I was going to call you; I was just trying to get this money together so you and my children would never have to worry about anything." Spyda started kissing on Linda in an attempt to calm her down. Although he loved Linda, most of his time was dedicated to the streets. "Come on, ma, you know I don't like you out here like this." Spyda walked Linda back across the street to her car and they both got inside.

As Spyda sat in the car kicking it with Linda, he saw three dudes with red bandanas run pass the car and stop in the middle of the street. Just then, they opened fire on Hunt, Chuck, and the rest of the crew.

"Oh shit!" Spyda pushed Linda down in the seat as they heard the constant firing of guns like they were right on top of them. "Shut the fuck up!" Spyda whispered in Linda's ear when she released a blood-curdling scream.

The gunmen never noticed them in the car and Spyda wanted it to stay that way. As soon as the gunshots ceased, Spyda heard the patting of feet as they ran from the scene. After raising his head, he noticed the three bodies.

"Oh, no!" Spyda yelled as he jumped out of the car and ran over to Chuck and Hunt, who were both lying on the ground bleeding from the face and head. He automatically knew Hunt had expired, but Chuck was still breathing. "Somebody call an ambulance!" Spyda screamed as he cradled Chuck in his arms. The other workers started gathering around while Lil' Murder ran into the corner store and told the storeowner to call the ambulance.

"Yo, it was them Blood niggas from the new side," one of the workers called out.

Chuck died before the ambulance arrived. Looking up, Spyda saw Linda standing over him, crying.

"Linda, page Rashawn and tell him that nigga Butter Bean made a move on us."

Linda left immediately, jumping into her car and pulling off.

* * * * *

Brian drove while Summer laid back listening to Amerie's CD. She was in deep thought. She and Brian were on their way to the hotel. Both were nervous about being with each other, but both wanted this just as much as the other. Suddenly, they were snapped out of their individual thoughts by a big bang and their heads being jerked back.

"Oh God! Brian, what was that?" Summer asked as they both turned around.

"Somebody hit us from the back. Are you alright?"

"Yes."

"Hold on, stay in the truck." As Brian exited the vehicle, Summer looked out the rearview mirror. Three men got out of a black-colored car that had rammed into the back of them. Then, all of a sudden, Brian started tussling with the men before everything came to a halt.

BANG! BANG! BANG!

Summer watched Brian fall to the ground. Everything seemed to have stopped for a tenth of a second before the passenger door was snatched open and Summer was dragged from the car. The men stripped her of her jewelry as they jumped in Brian's truck and pulled off, followed by the car they were driving in.

"Oh my God! Brian! No! Please God, No!" Summer ran over to Brian, who had been hit twice in the chest. "Somebody please help me!" Summer screamed as she cuddled Brian tight in her arms, her voice ECHOEING in the distance of the summer's night.

* * * * *

"Oh Rashawn! Yes, right there! Yes, this pussy is yours to do whatever you want with it." Destiny moaned in pleasure with Rashawn's face buried between her legs. She held a tight grip on his head, making sure he continued to focus on her spot.

"Yesss, Rashawn!" Destiny murmured as his platinum tongue explored her super sensitive clitoris. As Rashawn concentrated on Destiny's clitoris, he used his pointer and middle finger to penetrate the interior of her womanhood.

"Oh Yesss! Yesss!" Destiny felt herself on the verge of cumming for a third time. She could no longer hold off. One of the main reasons Destiny only dealt with older men was because to her they were more experienced with pleasuring a woman and most put the woman's feelings first, whereas the young boys just wanted some head and a quick fuck.

Destiny lost her breath as Rashawn's tongue tapped at her clit, sending surges through her entire body, from her center and out to the tips of her toes and fingers. He continued to make small circles with her clitoris as he plunged both fingers in and out of her faster and faster. While tasting her love juices in his mouth, he murmured non-verbal words that sent vibrations swelling throughout her body echoing with pleasure.

BUZZZZZZ...BUZZZZZZ...BUZZZZZZZ...

Their BlackBerry's went off simultaneously.

"Don't answer it, daddy," Destiny pleaded with Rashawn as she tried to hold him from getting up.

"Hold up, baby girl; you know I have to get that."

Rashawn stood and snatched his BlackBerry off of the counter. Destiny rolled over and did the same thing while Rashawn called back whoever had called. Noticing it was a call from home, she didn't bother calling back, figuring it to be her grandmother trying to find out where she was. Destiny placed the BlackBerry on the nightstand as she laid back down to wait for Rashawn to finish what he had started. While looking at Rashawn while he spoke on the phone, she saw the puzzled look on his face and knew something had happened. She did her best to ear hustle, but was only able to catch the end part of what he said before he hung up the cell phone.

"Baby, is everything a'ight?" Destiny asked as she sat up in the bed and hugged Rashawn around his neck while she licked his ear. Rashawn pushed her off of him as he stood up and started getting dressed.

"Come on, we got to go. They just killed my boys Chuck and Hunt in the Pj's."

"Oh no!" Destiny jumped out the bed and started getting dressed. She had known Hunt and Chuck for years. Chuck use to date her best friend Kimba before she died of cancer.

As Destiny dressed, her BlackBerry went off. It was home again. Ignoring the call, Destiny turned her two-way off as her and Rashawn left out the door.

* * * * *

By the time the police and ambulance arrived, Summer was sitting in the middle of the street in shock covered in Brian's blood with him tightly clutched in her arms. The paramedics rushed to start working on Brian, but he had already died.

Before taking his last breath, he told Summer to be strong and take the world by storm. Summer couldn't figure out what he had meant, but that was the last thing on her mind at the present. She had witnessed the man she was willing to spend the rest of her life with murdered in cold blood. Now, she had lost three important people in her life to senseless murders. As she held Brian in her arms and felt the life drain from his body, she thought about her own parents' murder. The world was cold and with each passing day, her heart was becoming just as cold.

* * * * *

Spyda told Rashawn to meet him at the crib they had down the block from the Pj's. There was still police and ambulance activity in front of their building as Rashawn made a left on the corner and headed for the Honeycomb Hideout, their little fuck house.

After pulling up in front of the house, he turned to Destiny to tell her that he'd be right back, when from the corner of his eye he spotted two figures running from behind a van parked in front of them as they started firing into the car. Without thinking, Rashawn pushed Destiny down into the seats and shielded her. Destiny screamed as she felt every time a slug hit Rashawn, his body shaking from the impact of each bullet. The two men continued to fire into the car until both of their guns were emptied. Then, they threw their weapons to the ground and ran off.

When Destiny felt it was okay to pick her head up, she called out to Rashawn, but got no response. "Oh God!

No! Please No!" Destiny started screaming, but what scared her most was she recognized both the shooters who had looked her dead in the face. She couldn't believe what just happened and by who. Destiny jumped out of the car and ran.

* * * * *

RING...RING...RING...
"Yo! Talk to me."
"We just hit 'em up about five minutes ago."
"That's good; come see me."
"But we have a problem."
"What type of problem?"
"The bitch saw us and we wasn't able to kill her. She looked me right in the eyes."
"That's not good at all, but that's a problem that can be fixed. So handle it. Get her before she tells the police or has this whole thing backfired in our face. If anybody finds out we set this up, shit can get ugly."
"So what 'cha want us to do now?"
"Muthafucka, make right what the fuck y'all made wrong...and quick!"
"A'ight."
CLICK...

* * * * *

BING BONG...BING BONG...BING BONG...
Ms. Hardy sat up in her bed and looked at the clock. "Who in the hell is ringing that damn bell like that at two in the morning? If this girl lost her keys, I'ma kill her."

38

Ms. Hardy pulled herself from the bed and went downstairs to answer the door. She had been paging both girls since about midnight, but neither called her back. Ms. Hardy didn't worry about Summer, but Destiny, who was too much like her father and stayed in some type of trouble, was a different story. When Ms. Hardy looked out the peephole, she recognized both the boys who were at the door. She quickly opened the door, thinking something happened to Destiny.

"Is everythi. . ." Before she could finish her sentence, the two guys at the door rushed in with their guns drawn and threw her to the floor. "Eeeeii!" Ms. Hardy screamed as she hit the floor, banging her head against the coffee table on her way down. She looked at the two with fear and shock in her eyes. She couldn't believe what they were doing.

"Where's your granddaughter?" one of the men asked, placing the barrel of his gun to her head.

"I don't know. I thought she left with y'all," Ms. Hardy answered in a faint voice.

"Well, we have a message for her."

BANG!

Ms. Hardy died instantly as the other person scribbled on the wall *'This will be your outcome if you say anything to anybody.'* Both men ran from the house, jumped in the dark-colored car, and peeled off into the night.

* * * * *

When Destiny reached her block, she was out of breath and scared. She noticed the same men who had just killed Rashawn running out of her grandmother's house.

Knots formed in Destiny's stomach as she ducked behind a car. She hoped Summer had stayed out all night with Brian and that they didn't do anything to their grandmother. As Destiny watched the car turn the corner, she ran to the house.

"Ma!" Destiny called out as she entered the front door. "Oh my God! Nooooo!"

Destiny ran over to her grandmother who was lying lifeless in a pool of her own blood.

* * * * *

"Yo Son, I think I saw that bitch Destiny peeping from behind that car on the block. Swing back around the block and let's double check."

"Nigga, are you crazy? We'll get that bitch another time. We just bodied two people."

"Man, listen, we got to get that bitch now. She knows who we are. Remember, she saw our faces? We can't afford having this lil' bitch say anything to anyone. So just go around the block to make sure."

* * * * *

Destiny cried uncontrollably. Their grandmother was all they had, and now she was dead because of some two-faced niggas who were just smiling in her face. Thinking of Summer, she jumped up and ran to the phone to call her.

As Destiny reached the phone, she froze. The two dudes who shot Rashawn and killed her grandmother were standing in the doorway. She started screaming as she tried to run to the backdoor, but her efforts were cut short by an

40

impact that spun her around, dropping her to the floor. Feeling as though she had been hit with a sledge hammer, Destiny lay on the floor unable to move. Her mind told her to try to make a break for it, but her body wouldn't respond. The sharp pain in her lower back let her know she had been shot. Destiny began to cry as the men she knew as friends stood over her.

She whispered, "Why?"

"You don't know why, Destiny? It's nothing against you. You just was in the wrong place at the wrong time."

"Yeah, like P. Diddy said, *'it's all about the Benjamins, baby.'* Both men laughed as the shorter of the two raised his pistol. "It's not personal; it's business. Think of it like this, now we don't have to kill your sister. Your life for hers."

BLOU!

* * * * *

After failed attempts at trying to reach her grandmother and sister, a young detective agreed to give Summer a lift home. Still devastated, the image of Brian being gunned down in front of her haunted her thoughts. Even though emotionally exhausted, she could still tell the young officer, who didn't look much older than she, was attracted to her. Summer had a somewhat fond attraction to him, as well, but she wouldn't allow her thoughts to go there.

Detective Diekman was twenty-six years old and had been on the force for five years, being a detective for only one of those years. Being born and raised in Brooklyn gave Detective Diekman an edge; therefore, he was familiar with the happenings in the city. He was the younger brother of Butter Bean, and his two older brothers were serving life in prison for murder. Of all the males in his family, he was the outcast because he didn't follow in their footsteps of crime and gangbanging. When Diekman became a police officer, he disowned his brothers. Diekman grew up in Smurf village with his brothers, and when they joined the Bloods, he chose to do what was right in school and kept his distance.

Diekman had watched Summer and her sister grow into the prettiest girls in the hood. He had never physically met them, but he knew of them. Aware that they were both young, he still couldn't help but notice how pretty and well-developed they both were. Diekman knew Summer was the good one and that Destiny stayed in trouble and kept the company of Rashawn, another thug who grew up in the same Pj's as he did. Although seven years older than Summer, he wished he had met her on different terms. During the ride to Summer's house, Diekman tried having small conversation with her. He even gave Summer a card and told her if she ever needed someone to talk to all she had to do was call.

When Diekman pulled up in front of Summer's house, the front door was wide open. This immediately caused suspicion amongst them both.

"Do y'all usually keep y'all front door wide open at this time of morning?" Diekman asked as he shut off the engine of the unmarked car.

"In this neighbor?! Hell No!"

"That's what I thought. You stay put while I go check it out." Diekman got out of the car and pulled his weapon out from his waistband as he approached the front door. As soon as he entered the house, he froze. "Oh my God!" Diekman's heart skipped a beat from the sight.

Before he could turn around, he felt Summer's presence behind him.

"Nooooo!" she screamed.

Diekman grabbed Summer and prevented her from going further into the house. However, once she entered that doorway, her life changed forever.

Chapter 3
Awaken The Sleeping Beauty

Three months later…

    Summer was taken to the hospital the night of the murders and admitted to the psychiatric ward where she has been ever since. Seeing her sister and grandmother lying in their blood was too much for her to comprehend. She cut herself off from the outside world and became a prisoner of her emotions. For months, Summer was non-responsive to any of the treatment and therapy of the doctors. Remaining motionless, she just sat and stared into nothingness with a blank look. She had to be fed intravenously because she wouldn't eat or drink; her desire to live was gone. Detective Diekman made it his business to visit Summer three times a week every month she had been there, but each visit was the same as the last. She just sat in her chair staring into nothingness.

    Diekman continued investigating the homicides of Ms. Hardy and Destiny. They learned the murders were all connected with Rashawn's murder. A witness to Rashawn's shooting told the police that they saw a young lady run from Rashawn's car after the shooting, and the police matched Destiny's fingerprints with prints found in Rashawn's car. As far as Brian's murder, the police pulled over the suspected killers in Brian's truck that night at a Burger King drive-thru and a gun battle between the carjackers and the police broke out, ending with one cop shot in the face and all occupants of the stolen vehicle dead. It was said they tried to surrender by dropping their weapons, but the police shot down the unarmed men in cold blood. The police retrieved Rashawn's truck and the gun used to murder Rashawn. The case was opened and closed that night.

Today was Sumner's 18th birthday, and Diekman planned to spend the day with her. When Diekman entered Summer's room, she was already dressed and sitting in her chair staring out the window. Summer still was as beautiful as ever, even though she had lost a lot of weight due to the fact she hadn't eaten in three months. Diekman paid one of the females who worked at the hospital to do Summer's hair every week and to make sure she was properly bathed and clothed. Diekman really felt bad for Summer and wanted to help her in anyway he could, not to mention his attraction to Summer. He knew she felt alone, which was one of the reasons he continued to visit her. He wanted her to know she wasn't alone.

Upon entering, he held in one hand a bouquet of flowers for her birthday and in the other, a plate of food. Whenever Diekman visited, he always brought her food. The doctors encouraged Diekman to try to get her to eat solid food.

"Hey, Beautiful. Happy birthday!" Diekman placed the flowers on Summer's lap and gave her a kiss on the cheek. He then sat the food on the stand at the foot of her bed. "I brought you some macaroni and cheese with fried chicken. I cooked it myself. Are you going to eat for me today?" Summer continued to stare out the window without blinking an eye to acknowledge Diekman's presence. Diekman pulled up a chair next to her.

"Listen, Summer, I've been coming here to visit you three times a week since you've been here. I have sat and spoke with you, and you've yet to respond to me. I can't say that I know what you're going through because I don't, but I'm willing to help you through it. I know you can hear me, so don't give up. You have a lot to live for. You have to live for Destiny; you have to live for your parents; you have to live for your grandmother, Brian, and most of all, you must live for Summer. You are here and your family will live on through you. If you give up, then they die. You deserve to live. I know it doesn't seem like it, but God spared your life for a reason, and only you and He know the reason. I've watched you and your sister grow up over the years, and I know you're stronger than this. You must find the strength within. I haven't given up on you, so please don't give up on yourself." Diekman leaned over and once again kissed Summer on her forehead. "I've been here with you every step of the way, and I think I'm falling in love with you. I need you! Summer, I'm on the job right now, but I will be back tomorrow."

Diekman turned and left out the room. What Diekman didn't notice was the tears forming at the corners of Summer's eyes. This was the first time Summer responded to anything since that night.

* * * * *

In the streets, it was business as usual. The war between the two sides of the Pj's had thickened. Rumors were causing a lot of uproar. It was said that Rashawn was murdered by Butter Bean and his crew of Bloods. It was also said that Rashawn's death was a result of a mob hit because he owed them some money. The recent rumor was that Spyda set Rashawn up so he could take over his business because Spyda was sick of being Rashawn's "yes man." At the same time, Spyda did take over where Rashawn left off, and made it his business to lay everything that was "dripping" down. "Dripping" is what they called a person who wore all red and belonged to the Blood set.

Spyda wanted Butter Bean and his Bloods out of the way so he could control both sides of the projects. Spyda had just gotten a new connect and the supply was bigger. With a greater demand to move the drugs, he had to try to squash the competition. Spyda, who was once the "yes man", was now *the man*. The difference between him and Rashawn was that Spyda stayed on the grind with the workers and soldiers in the streets. They had more respect for Spyda because he didn't put himself on a higher level than his workers. He would never ask them to do something he wouldn't do.

The night after the shooting, Spyda's girl had a baby boy, so he was determined to get rich off that Brooklyn drug money even if it meant stepping on a few toes. He moved his baby's mother to Queens, but he still had a down-low crib in Brooklyn.

Spyda put his boys Justice and Big Ruben on as his top men. Big Ruben was a trigger-happy slim cat. They called him Big Ruben because when it came to putting in that gun play, he was as big as anybody. As a matter of fact, when Big Ruben had a gun in his hand, he became a giant. He never hesitated to use it when he pulled it out, which was often. That was one of the reasons Rashawn didn't fuck with Big Ruben, because he was too trigger happy, and that kind of heat made it hard for them to get money. Homicide stayed looking for Big Ruben. All they ever had on him was hearsay, but they never had anybody that could put Big Ruben at the scene of a murder. Spyda had sent Justice to Ohio. He also sent Judy, a lil dyke broad from the projects, with him. Justice use to be a five percenter until he was exiled for setting up one of the brothers to get robbed and murdered, which was one of the reasons Justice couldn't come back to New York. When he was in New York, he had to creep because he had a whole nation out to kill him, and when in Brooklyn, he didn't leave the Pj's.

The week after Rashawn's murder, Sha was released from prison after serving her time. She learned of Rashawn's murder while in jail, and as soon as she hit the streets, she stepped to Spyda. Spyda blessed her with money and told her that he had her covered. Immediately, they became an item.

Prison did wonders for Sha. Besides making her coldhearted and ruthless, the 1600 crunches a day had her thighs, legs, and ass on one thousand. She was thin in the waist, a dime in the face, short with a body to kill for, and had an attitude like a straight killer. Street smart and wise, she knew she had to move with what was popping, so she quickly got with Spyda and was willing to move with him in order to gain his complete trust. Not to mention, she fucked his brains out to make him fall in love with the pussy so she could get what she wanted out of him. Sha knew how to use her sex, body, and mind to get what she desired. Little did Spyda know, but Sha was still loyal to Rashawn even in death, and she wanted to know if the rumors were true. She knew she would have to gain Spyda's complete trust for her to get that information from

48

him. And if Spyda had crossed Rashawn, she would make him pay for his betrayal.

While Spyda stood in front of the building with about fifteen of his soldiers, Big Ruben pointed at a Range that had stopped out. "Spyda, heads up." Big Ruben didn't know who was in the truck because all the windows were tinted, but Spyda knew. Sha had gone and got Rashawn's Range that was shot up out the shop. With the Range being in her name, Rashawn's mother couldn't take it. Nor could his mother claim ownership of the house Rashawn had purchased before Sha got locked up.

"Yo, Dog, who's that?" Big Ruben asked as most of the workers pulled out their heat, ready for anything.

"Oh nah, y'all, that's Sha," Spyda replied while walking over to the vehicle and jumping in. "Yo, what's up, ma? You almost got dealt with." Spyda leaned over and gave Sha a kiss. "What brings you out here? Spying on me?"

"Something like that. I'm just making sure you don't have your baby mama or none of them lil' chicken head bitches around you."

"Come on, ma, you know it ain't like that."

"Yeah, okay, Spyda, that's what you tell me. No, but seriously, I was on my way to the soul food restaurant and wanted to know if you wanted anything?"

"You know I do. A nigga is starving. This chronic got me wanting to eat like crazy."

"Daddy, let me get some of that shit you smoking," Sha pleaded.

"Yeah, right, so your ass can get violated? Never would I let you do that."

"Just testing to see how much you really care about me."

"Come on, girl. I think I done did the dummy move and fell in love with you," Spyda said as he leaned over and placed his hand under her dress while she drove.

"Yeah, tell me anything. You're just in love with how I work it." Sha pulled Spyda's hand from in between her thighs. "What 'cha trying to do, boy, make me crash?"

"Never that. I just wanted to touch what's mine."

"What do you want to eat?"

"Do you have to ask?"

"I'm talking about food from the restaurant."

"Oh okay, in that case, get me a large order of macaroni and cheese with fried whitey."

"What time are you coming to my house tonight, or is tonight your night to go to your bitch's house?"

"Come on, Sha, don't act like that. You know I still got to take care of my children."

"Yeah, but what's taking care of your children have to do with you still fucking with your baby's mama?" Sha rolled her eyes as she focused on the road. Sha played like she didn't want Spyda fucking with his baby's mother, but on the real, she didn't care because she had another man, as well. She was only using Spyda to get to the truth.

"Sha, don't start this shit. You knew the situation before we got together. I've been with Linda before you went to prison. So, don't start acting crazy now."

"Yeah, Spyda, that was before I started falling in love with you. I was just coming home from prison and fiendin' for a man, but now my emotions bother me every time I think of you with that bitch. I want you for myself. You don't have to share me with nobody else, so why do I have to share you?" Sha reached over and started rubbing up the side of Spyda's leg until she felt his manhood become erect. With one motion, she unzipped his pants, pulled out his cock, and started jerking him off. Spyda just laid his head back and enjoyed the pleasure of Sha's hand. As soon as Sha felt Spyda's manhood stiffen, as if he was about to cum, she stopped. "Look at your nasty butt. You was ready to bust off in my car," Sha said as she put Spyda's cock back into his pants.

"Hell yeah, you had a nigga in a zone. After we cop this food, it's time for us to rush back to your crib so I can hit that. What you trying to do to a nigga, give me blue balls?"

"Spyda, I want you to be careful," she said, changing the subject. "I heard them niggas from the new side just brought a few guys from upstate Albany. Y'all don't know how those niggas look, so y'all got to be careful."

"How you know this?"

"My girl Starkia fucks with one of them niggas. I just drove by there and they had like thirty muthafuckas out in front of their building."

"Ma, what you doing driving through there like that? What I tell you? This shit ain't no game. Them bum ass niggas might want to try and get at you because they too scared to come at me."

"Come on, Spyda, I'm not new to this game. I just served five years for this shit and held my head. That shit just made my heart more cold and vicious. I want those niggas just as much as you do."

"I feel you, Boo. Just have a lil' patience and all them niggas is going to pay. As for that heart of yours being cold, I have something that can warm it up." Spyda rubbed Sha's thighs until he had his hand up the Coogi dress she was wearing. He then licked his lips as he slid Sha's thong to the side and started fingering her.

"Boy, I told you to stop. Now come on." Sha moved Spyda's hand as she parked in front of the restaurant. As they were walking into the restaurant, Dollar Bill was coming out.

"Hey, what's up, Sha?"

"Aye, what's going on, Dollar Bill?" Sha gave Dollar Bill a hug and entered the restaurant.

"Dollar muthafuckin' Bill! What's poppin', cat daddy?" Spyda gave him a pound. Dollar Bill was an old timer from the old side of the projects.

"Spyda! What's up, baby? Man, I should be asking you what's poppin'. The word on these streets is that you and your crew is what's happening now since my lil' man Rashawn was hit up."

"You know how the old side rocks from when you and your crew use to run shit."

"Yeah, lil' nigga, don't get it fucked up, though. We still run shit."

"Dollar Bill, please! Most of them niggas is either in jail, dead, or smoked out, and your old ass probably got life parole. So, I know you ain't trying to get your hands dirty no more," Spyda said as he laughed.

"Like I said, young'n, don't get it fucked up." Dollar Bill pulled up his shirt, revealing his .40 caliber. "Nigga, I'm holding court in the streets. You need to give a nigga a job. You already know my specialty…that 1-8-7, baby! I've been home for a week, and it's hard for a nigga."

"Yo, Dollar, I'ma get at you in a couple of days." Spyda took out a piece of paper and wrote his number down. "Call me at the end of the week. I should have something for you to do." Spyda handed Dollar Bill the piece of paper, then pulled out a mitt, peeled three crisp hundreds off the top of the stack of money, and handed it to Dollar. "Make sure you call me, man."

"You know it, baby. Good lookin' out." Dollar Bill gave Spyda a pound, and then Spyda went into the restaurant. Sha had already ordered the food and was waiting.

"Spyda, I hope you ain't fuckin' with that nigga. You know he's worse than that nigga Big Ruben. Trouble seems to follow him. He hasn't spent a full summer, or should I say a full season, out of prison since I was about eight years old. Since I've known Dollar Bill, he's been in and out of prison. When you don't see him for awhile, you know he's in prison."

"Yeah, and a lot of niggas feel safe when Dollar Bill is on lockdown. That's the type of nigga I need with my crew. A muthafucka that people is scared to breathe around."

"Yeah, Spyda, that use to be true, but these young boys nowadays won't hesitate to put one in him. Shit changed from when we were growing up and cats like Dollar Bill were feared."

"Yeah, you right, and I'm one of them young niggas that won't think twice about putting one of these hot ones in a nigga's ass."

"That's why I'm so attracted to you. I need a thug. A gentleman ain't going to do it for me."

After Sha paid for their food, they left out the restaurant.

* * * * *

"Yo, Butter, why you still fucking with that bitch Sha? She fucks with that nigga Spyda."

"Blood, you don't think I know what I'm doing? I'ma 'bout to peel that nigga Spyda's cap back and he don't even know it's coming. Throughout history, wars have been won because niggas was weak for bitches. How do you think in the bible they found out that Samson's strength was his hair? They sent a bitch at the nigga, and he told it all. In chess, once you catch a King's Queen, his whole game is fucked up. You got to learn that a Queen is just a pawn with fancy moves, and once you manipulate that woman's mind the weak ass nigga will follow. Remember, that nigga is weak. First of all, we know it wasn't us that hit Rashawn up. Although we would have wanted to, it was that nigga's doing. And that's the problem she has with the nigga. She knows Spyda set Rashawn up, too. So all we got to do is play our position and the mouse is going to lead the cat right where we want him. That nigga wants everybody to think we hit up Rashawn. He's smart. He waited until we made our move on the old side when we hit those niggas Chuck and Hunt up. Then, he made his move and hit that nigga Rashawn and his bitch whereas it would seem like we did the hit. It was a smart move, but I was one step ahead of the nigga. When I found out Sha was coming home, I had one of the Bloodettes in Danbury step to her and explain what was going down and how the nigga Spyda crossed her man. Of course she didn't want to believe it, so she's trying to get the nigga to admit to it." Butter Bean passed Black Supreme the dust blunt he was smoking.

Black Supreme was from the other side of Brooklyn. He lived in Brownsville, but he and Butter Bean became close up north in the Elmira State Prison. Black Supreme was born God body, but became a Blood in prison. He kept the name because he felt the name was gangsta. In prison, Black Supreme and Butter Bean had a beef with some Spanish cats. They were the only Bloods in the yard at the time and they held their own. Ever since, they have been mad tight.

"Yo, Damu, you know what kinda scares me a little?"

"What's that, Blood?"

"Your brother's been around here fucking with the Bloods kinda hard. He thinks we had something to do with that Rashawn shit and that bitch Destiny's murder. You need to talk to the nigga."

"Yo, Blood, you know I don't fuck with the police."

"Yeah, but Diekman is your lil' brother."

"Fuck that nigga! Blood is my Damu. That nigga stopped being my brother when he became police. Fuck that nigga!" Butter Bean guzzled some Henny from the bottle they were drinking. Every time somebody mentioned his brother being the police, he felt knots in his stomach. "Yo, Blood, go check on them niggas out front and make sure everything is good for tonight."

"A'ight, fam." Black Supreme passed Butter Bean the blunt and left out the house. Butter Bean looked at his watch; it was 11 p.m. He wanted some pussy. Butter had plenty of shorties he could call, but he wanted Sha. Picking up the phone, he paged her.

* * * * *

As soon as she and Spyda finished eating, they both stripped. When Spyda peeled off Sha's clothes, his manhood immediately stood at attention. She had a body many women would die for, with curves in all the right places. Her breasts were firm and full, and she had no cellulite anywhere, just pure thickness.

Spyda had Sha bent over the couch, with her forearms and knees supporting her body weight and her ass raised in the air while he hammered her from behind. She moaned and grunted loud enough for the neighbors to hear. As Spyda fucked Sha like he never was going to get to hit it again, Sha's pager sounded. She reached over, grabbed the pager while Spyda continued to handle his business, and turned it off without bothering to look to see who was calling. At that moment, she didn't really care. She was too busy enjoying what Spyda was doing to her womanhood. If it turned out that Spyda was behind setting Rashawn up, she was going to miss his sex, but for betrayal, he would have to die.

* * * * *

When Diekman reached home that night, he turned on his Luther CD and laid back. He was exhausted and the case was going nowhere. All he had was a bunch of hearsay. His brother's name came up, and he wouldn't hesitate to lock Butter up if he turned out to be responsible for the murders. One minute, the streets were saying Butter and his crew of Bloods did the hit, and then they were saying Spyda had set the whole thing up so he could take over Rashawn's drug empire. Diekman had yet to bring any of them in for questioning, but was considering snatching up Butter and Spyda within the next few days.

Diekman had dosed off on the couch when he was awakened by a light tap at his door. "Who in the hell could be at my door this time of the night?" he asked himself while jumping up and walking to the door. When he looked through the peephole, he couldn't believe his eyes.

Diekman snatched his door open and froze. Summer stood holding the flowers and the plate of food he had left for her.

"Are you hungry?" Summer asked as tears ran down her face. Diekman hurried her in and hugged her.

"Summer, are you alright?" Diekman couldn't believe she had actually spoken.

"No, I'm hungry," Summer responded, while trying to give him a little smile.

That night, Diekman comforted Summer and held her in his arms as she rested. The next morning, she told him that she remembered every visit and everything he had said to her. She thanked him for being there for her when she needed him and for helping her back to reality. Afterwards, they made passionate love.

Chapter 4
Life Goes On

Later that evening, Diekman drove Summer to her house, which Penny and Cookie took care of while she was hospitalized. Ms. Hardy and Destiny's insurance policies paid for the funeral expenses, as well as any bills.

"Diekman, I don't know how I'll ever be able to repay you for everything you have done for me in my time of need. You have been a guardian angel." Summer looked into Diekman's eyes as he stood in the doorway.

"You have already thanked me enough just by showing up at my door last night. Not to mention the beautiful lovemaking this morning. What better way for a person to show their gratitude than giving themselves to another person? Man! I should be thanking you. By the way, how did you know where I lived?"

"Officer Diekman, did you forget that you gave me your card that night at the precinct?"

"Summer, please call me Justin. Officer Diekman is too formal."

"Justin? That's a beautiful name. Who named you that?"

"I'm named after my grandfather. His name was Justin Diekman, as well."

"Okay, Justin, no more Diekman."

"That's what I'm talking about. You make Justin sound so sexy coming from your mouth."

"Justin, have the police ever found out who was responsible for my sister and grandmother's deaths?" Summer asked, becoming more serious.

"No, not yet, Summer, but I'm on the case. I'm not giving up until I find and jail all the parties involved. Believe and trust me, Summer. They will be apprehended."

Justin neglected to tell Summer that his older brother Butter Bean was a suspect in the murders. He felt it wasn't yet time to tell Summer that information, because as of now, it was just hearsay along with a few other names they both knew. "But we have a few leads we're working on, and as soon as I know something, you will."

"What about Brian's murder?"

"They were apprehended that night at a Burger King drive-thru. When the police approached the vehicle, the suspects felt like they should press their luck and shoot it out with the police."

"Was anybody hurt?"

"An officer was shot in the face, but he lived. As for the suspects, they were all killed. Listen, Summer, are you going to be alright? I have to go to work, but I'll be back to check on you when I get off."

"Yes, Justin, I'm doing a lot better. I just had to come to grips with the reality of losing everybody that I had. Thanks to you, I know I have to live for them now. I'm going to take a long, hot bath, relax, and maybe call Cookie and Penny to come keep me company."

"Okay, so I'll see you later?"

"Yes." Summer leaned in and gave Justin a kiss before he returned to his car. Immediately after closing the door, Summer called Cookie and Penny, remembering how they were faithful in visiting her in the hospital. Those two, along with Justin, continued to come to the hospital even though she wouldn't acknowledge their presence. Still, Summer knew they understood what she was going through.

* * * * *

Butter Bean and Black Supreme stood in front of the game room Butter Bean owned, kicking it to two shorties that they had stopped in a brand new, cherry apple Range Rover. When Sha pulled up in a cab, she called out the window, "Butter!" Butter Bean turned around with a stupid look on his face when he recognized the voice. He was expecting Sha to beef about being all up in the two girls' faces, but she didn't. Instead, she calmly called him over to the cab.

Butter walked off and left the girl standing with Black Supreme and the other girl. "Hey, what's up, Sha? I've been trying to reach you all night. Why haven't you answered your cell phone?"

"I had the battery charging," she lied. "I'm on my way to your house now. How long are you going to be?"

"I'll meet you there in five minutes. I have to take care of some business with my two new carriers, and then I'm on my way." Butter felt like he had to lie about who the two girls were.

"Alright, I'll be waiting." Sha rolled the window back up as the cab pulled off.

Butter walked back over to where Black Supreme and the two girls were standing. As soon as he stepped foot on the sidewalk, two unmarked cars pulled up and stopped right in front of him. Five plainclothes detectives jumped out with their weapons drawn.

"Don't move, dickhead! Police!"

"Yo! What the fuck is this about?" Before Butter could get a chance to do or say anything else, one detective swept him off his feet and slammed him to the concrete. At the same time, the other detective threw Black Supreme to the ground, while the others slammed the two ladies up against the wall and patted them down.

"Get your muthafuckin' hands off me, bitch!" Butter screamed as he struggled with the two detectives who had their knees in his back while handcuffing him.

"Officers, what's the problem?" Black Supreme asked in a respectful manner as the detective lifted him off the ground after checking him for weapons.

A short officer told Black Supreme and the girls to leave once they finished frisking them. "Man, I'm not going nowhere until I know what y'all doing to my homeboy," Black Supreme replied as the two girls hurried off without saying a peep.

"Oh, you don't wanna leave without your homeboy, huh?" the officer said as he pushed Black Supreme. "Do you want me to lock your ass up with him?"

"For what?"

"First of all, you're obstructing justice, so leave now."

Knowing he was on the run from a parole violation, Black Supreme didn't want to press it. So, without saying anything else, he walked off as he watched Butter struggle with the two detectives.

"Ahhh! Y'all are breaking my fucking arm!" Butter Bean complained as the detectives lifted him by the handcuffs, bending back his arms.

"Shut up and stop crying! You weren't crying when you murdered that girl and her grandmother."

"What?! Man, I didn't murder nobody! I don't know what the fuck y'all talking about."

"Yeah, okay, we'll see." The officers proceeded to read him the Miranda rights before throwing him into the back of the white police van that had pulled up.

*   *   *   *   *

Spyda had just pulled in front of Linda's house in Queens when he noticed a dark green, Lincoln Town Car parked across the street with tinted windows. Not liking the vibe he felt, he threw the car back in drive. Out of the blue, a car came towards him, driving in the wrong direction. As the doors of the town car swung open, four officers jumped out and ran towards him, pointing their weapons and yelling for him to turn the car off. Before Spyda knew what was happening, he was being pulled through the window of his car and slammed to the ground.

"Freeze! Police! Don't fucking move!"

Linda came running out the house when she heard all the commotion. "What are y'all doing to him? Let him go!" Linda ran up to the police and started trying to pull them off of Spyda, who was laying on the ground facedown with three officers on top of him. One of the three officers spun off of him and grabbed Linda in a chokehold to restrain her.

"Listen! If you don't want to get arrested with this piece of shit, I advise you to back off, calm down, and let the officers do their job."

Linda immediately calmed down, and the officer released her.

* * * * *

After getting off the phone with Cookie and Penny, Summer jumped in the shower. As her mind traveled to the last time she was in the house the night of the murders, tears started forming in the corner of her eyes. Summer wiped her tears away, refusing to let them fall.

I promised myself that I wouldn't cry another tear until I find out who's responsible for the death of my loved ones. Summer wouldn't allow herself to feel sorry, only determined to get even. "I failed you, Mommy. I promised I would always take care of my little sister, but I let her get murdered. I broke my promise to Mommy, Destiny, but I won't break my promise to you. I will make them pay for what they did to you and Grandma. I won't rest nor will I shed a tear until my promise is fulfilled."

For the last couple of months, the only conversation Summer had been having was with her mother and sister. Their conversations had been so deep that she had cut the outside world off. These conversations had become her reality. The only other voice Summer paid attention to was that of Justin Diekman the day of her birthday. Yes, Summer remembered every conversation Justin, Penny, and Cookie held when they came to visit her, but her thoughts were always elsewhere, her mind and heart with her deceased family.

Summer now felt obligated to get whoever was responsible. The blood of all parties involved would be the only way their souls would be able to rest in peace. Summer struggled with the good in her conscious, but this was the only way she could find out who's who and what's what. She knew she would have to use Justin for whatever info he had without letting her feelings get involved.

As soon as Summer finished drying off and dressing, she made herself a cup of hot chocolate and warmed a Danish while listening to her grandmother's Kirk Franklyn CD. Before she knew, she had dozed off.

* * * * *

"Mommy, Summer won't share with me. I dropped all of my potato chips and Summer won't give me none of hers."

Lyric picked up her youngest daughter and kissed her on the cheek. "Awww! Come on, baby, let's go see why your big sister is being stingy to the baby." Lyric walked into the girls' room with Destiny at her side. Summer was sitting in front of their TV, eating her chips. "Summer!" Summer quickly turned around with a bothered look on her face, as if she knew she had done wrong.

"Yes, Mommy?" she replied with the most innocent look on her face.

"What seems to be the problem? Did your little sister drop her potato chips?"

"Yes."

"Did you offer to share yours with her?"

"No."

"And why not? What do we teach y'all about making sure each other are always good, and if one has but the other doesn't have, that means you both should have, even if y'all have to share the little you do have?" Lyric and Destiny sat down beside Summer.

"Yes, Mommy, I know." Summer passed Destiny the other half of the bag of chips. "I was only teasing her. I saved her half. Destiny, this is for you."

"Thank you, Summer." Destiny gave her sister a hug as she accepted the half bag of chips.

Lyric hugged her two girls tightly together. "Y'all know Mommy loves y'all more than anything in the whole world."

"Even Daddy, Mommy?" Destiny asked.

"I love y'all all the same. It's just that the love Mommy and Daddy share for each other is a little different than the love Mommy and Daddy share for their children."

"Is that why you and Daddy be in the room with y'all door closed, and you be making them noises because you and Daddy love each other so much?" Summer asked as her and Destiny smiled at each other. Lyric blushed from the question asked by her nine-year-old.

"Yes, baby, something like that. But this ain't about me and Daddy right now." Lyric quickly changed the conversation and switched it back on them. "It's about you and your sister. Summer, you are the oldest, and I want you to promise Mommy that you will always take care of your sister and never let nothing happen to her. Can you promise Mommy that?"

"Yes, Mommy, I promise. I love my little sister."

"I love you, too, Summer. Here, I don't want all of your chips." Destiny passed the bag of chips back to her sister.

"That's what Mommy likes to see. Regardless of whom or what, you girls will always have each other." Lyric tried her best to instill family values in the girls and a bond in each other that would be unbreakable. "You girls make sure y'all stick together forever and never let anything come between y'all, not even death. I love y'all." Lyric leaned over and gave both girls kisses. "Now, I want y'all to behave for Grandma tonight. Daddy is on his way

with her. She's going to baby sit tonight while me and Daddy go out for a while."

"Mommy, are you really going to be on the radio and TV singing?"

"Yes, Destiny, that's why your father is taking me out tonight, so we can celebrate the signing of my record contract."

"Are we going to be rich, Mommy?" Summer's face lit up like the morning star.

"I sure hope so, baby, but that all depends on how well the people like Mommy singing."

"I like the way you sing, Mommy. You sing better than Mary J. Blige."

"Awww, baby, that means a lot to Mommy."

"So, we are going to be rich because Mary J. Blige is rich and you sing better than her." Lyric just smiled at her two precious jewels as Be-Real and Ms. Hardy walked in the door.

"Grandma!" both girls screamed as they charged into her arms.

"Baby, are you ready?" Be-Real put Ms. Hardy's bag down and kissed Lyric.

"Yes, but let me just write down our cell phone number on the fridge for the girls in case they have to call us." Lyric walked into the kitchen.

"Okay, you two, I want y'all to behave for Grandma, and no fighting."

"Okay, Daddy," the girls said in unison.

"If y'all be good, when me and Mommy get back, we have a special treat for y'all."

"What is it, Daddy? Tell us," Summer said as they both jumped on their father, anxious.

"If I tell y'all, it won't be a surprise, would it? So y'all just have to behave yourselves until me and Mommy gets back."

"Okay, Daddy. We love you." The girls pulled their grandmother to the back to show her their room.

Lyric exited the kitchen. "You ready? Do you have the car keys?"

"Yes, Lyric, and it's your night. The sky's the limit. Whatever you desire is my command, my Queen. The question is not if I'm ready, the question is, is the world ready for my soulful Lyric?" Be-Real grabbed Lyric by the waist and pulled her close to him. "Let's make this night last forever...my last night before I have to share my Lyric with the rest of the world."

They embraced and kissed as if it was their last before leaving the house.

* * * * *

Summer jumped up off the couch when she heard keys in the door. She looked at the time. *Damn! I must have dozed off. It's already after ten o'clock,* Summer thought as she stood up and walked to the door. She knew it had to be Cookie and Penny, since they still had keys to the house. As soon as the front door opened, they all ran and embraced each other. It was as if they hadn't seen each other in years.

"Summer, you had us so worried," Cookie said while wiping away her tears.

"How are you feeling, Summer? One day, you're in a comatose state of mind, and the next day, you're home. Penny locked the door behind her.

"I know I had y'all worried, but the shock of that night got the best of me and it took a while before I realized I had to continue living for my sister. I'm doing much better now that my two best friends are here with me. Without y'all I don't know if I would have made it. I remember every visit, and I want to thank y'all for everything y'all have done for me. By the way, the house looks great." Summer hugged both girls once more.

"Girl, enough of all the mushy stuff. Let's get to the real. Who's that handsome young policeman you had coming to see you every other day? Girl, he's fine, and he helped with everything." They all walked over to the couch and took seats as Cookie pulled out a bag of weed.

"Cookie, when did you start smoking that stuff?"

"Summer, I was so stressed about your condition I started smoking weed after the funeral." After the mentioning of the funeral, the room grew quiet. Penny could see tears forming in Summer's eyes, but once again, Summer fought them off.

"I just want to thank y'all for everything. Y'all are the only family I have left."

"Come on, Summer, you don't have to tell us that. We're your girls. As a matter of fact, if you haven't noticed, I already done moved in on your butt," Cookie said as she started rolling the blunt. "I decided not to move with my moms and sistah. I'ma stay here with you until you kick me out."

"Shiiiit! Then you're here for good."

"Yeah, okay, now back to that fine officer from the hospital?" Penny asked

"Who? Detective Justin Diekman?"

"Girl, you know who we're talking about."

"Oh girl, he has been so supportive since that night. I met him after Brian was murdered. He is one of the homicide detectives on the case, and he is the one who brought me home that night."

"Girl, not only is he fine as hell, but he's also from around here. I remember seeing him a few times, but I can't remember from where." Cookie sparked the blunt.

"Penny, what happened to you going to college?"

"After what happened to you and everything with Destiny and your grandmother, my mind wasn't with school, so I'm a substitute teacher at the junior high school."

That night, Summer smoked weed for the first time. Once in a relaxed state, she told the girls of her plan to kill all the people who were involved with the murders of her sister and grandmother. The girls informed Summer of the rumors surfacing in the streets, and they agreed to help Summer get whoever was responsible, regardless of the sacrifices.

That night, they made a bond…UNTIL DEATH DO THEM PART.

* * * * *

Big Ruben and Justice rushed out the door and headed for Queens after Linda called and told them what had happened to Spyda. They called Sha and told her to go collect the money that was out while they went to see if Spyda would get a bail. Spyda had the majority of the money stashed at Linda's crib, and when Linda called, she sounded hysterical and saying crazy shit, so they wanted to get to her quick. As soon as they turned on Fulton, Justice noticed Black Supreme walking towards the projects like he was in a hurry.

"Yo, Ruben, ain't that that nigga Black Supreme right there?" Justice pointed towards Black Supreme who ducked into a shoe store.

"Yeah, that's that nigga. Let's get 'em."

* * * * *

Having walked all the way from East New York to the Sty, Black Supreme was out of breath. He wanted to jump in a cab, but realized the police had stolen the money he had in his pocket. He didn't wanna chance jumping the train turnstile or jumping out of a cab, because the way his luck was going he would get knocked for that stupid shit. So, he decided to walk.

"Oh shit!" Black Supreme spotted Big Ruben and Justice as they turned onto Fulton. "Damn! I knew I should have walked down Atlantic Avenue." Black Supreme ducked into a Payless Shoe Store and ran to the back.

"Hey! What are you doing? You can't be back here!" the store manager said as she followed behind him. Without hesitation, Black Supreme pulled out his heat and pointed it at the female's face.

"Shut the fuck up! Please, niggas is trying to kill me. If you keep quiet, you won't be hurt."

After entering the store, Big Ruben and Justice stopped and looked around. Black Supreme cocked back the hammer, ready to start blasting. He gestured to the frightened manager not to move or make a sound. Black Supreme peeped from the back as he heard them leave out the store.

Yeah, let them niggas go. I'll get those niggas tonight, Black Supreme said to himself while walking to the door to see if the coast was clear. When he peeped out the door, Big Ruben came from his blind side and pointed his piece at Black Supreme's head.

Boom...Boom...Boom...

Black Supreme's body dropped to the floor as blood poured from his head wound. Everybody in the store started screaming as they fell to the floor, praying they weren't next. The crowded Fulton Street erupted in chaos as people scattered from the sight of the two armed gunmen. Never once did anybody take the time to get a look at their faces. Big Ruben and Justice broke out, running with the crowd. As they pulled off, they saw the police run into the shoe store.

Chapter 5
The Shakedown

"Yo! What the fuck is going on? What's the problem? I don't know nothing about nothing." Butter sat in a room with a table and his hands handcuffed behind him, while one officer dressed in a suit sat across from him saying nothing. "Yo, where the fuck is Justin?"

Just as Butter asked the question, Detective Diekman walked into the room. As soon as their eyes met, Butter could feel the hatred building up. The hate he had for his younger brother was greater than the hate he had for Spyda and the cats from the old side.

"Hey, big brother, how are you holding up?" Justin asked as he took a seat on the opposite side of the table and passed his brother a Newport.

"How the fuck do you think I'm holding up? And don't address me as your brother. You've been dead to me ever since the day you put that bitch-ass badge on, nigga!" Butter bent over and accepted the Newport into his mouth as Justin lit it.

"Come on now, Mike, you're still my brother. We come from the same womb."

"Nigga, my name is Butter. We come from the same pussy but different dicks. And my daddy don't make no police, only gangstas." Butter looked into his brother's eyes and all he could think about was the times Justin's father, who at the time he thought was his father too, use to beat him, and Butter hated his brother even more.

"Well right now, big brother of mine, it's not about you and me. That's not why you're here. This is about the killing of Rashawn, Destiny, and her grandmother. Do you know anything about that, because your name keeps popping up? So why is that?"

"Come on, Justin, y'all know who's responsible for that shit, and y'all know me or my people didn't kill 'em. Y'all just on my dick because half the precinct was on Rashawn's payroll. Nigga, how much is them chumps paying you to lock up your own brother? Nigga, I'm ashamed that you came from the same womb as me."

"Come on, Mike, you know me better than that. I'm clean, and furthermore, we're the police."

"Exactly! That's what I'm talking about. Y'all the police, and y'all know who killed them people."

"The word is that you and your Bloods killed Chuck and Hunt, then hit up Rashawn. And since Destiny saw who did it, y'all made sure she wouldn't tell anybody."

"Come on, lil' bro, use your mind. Did I benefit from murdering Rashawn? Who did? Who's the man now? Y'all muthafuckas know I didn't have no parts of that shit, although I would have liked to have been the one that stuck it to that muthafucka."

"The word is that you and your lil' punk ass Blood clique is bringing all type of fire power from upstate."

"You know what, Justin? The punk ass Blood clique you're talking about is the same ones who protected your ass all these years, and the only reason you're still alive. That same punk ass Blood clique is what all of your brothers and uncles represent."

"Yeah, that same punk ass Blood clique is the reason most of them is dead or in jail now. The same direction you're headed in, if you don't slow down."

"Fuck you, punk! I've protected your punk ass all these years."

"Yeah, Mike, but once again, this is not about me and you."

Butter looked his lil' brother in the eyes. "Justin, if it wasn't for our mother, your ass wouldn't live to see tomorrow."

"Are you threatening a police officer? You know I can throw your ass in jail for that. Furthermore, I'm not worried about your lil' Blood crew. Y'all have enough problems with the old side."

"Man, fuck you! Are y'all arresting me? Am I being charged with something? If not, let me the fuck go."

"No, you're not being charged with anything, and you will be let go. I just wanted to have a brother-to-brother talk with you. It's been a long time."

As Justin spoke to Butter, another officer entered the room and whispered something in Detective Diekman's ear, then turned and left. Justin looked at his brother and shook his head before speaking.

"Butter, it seems as if you and your Blood clique are having big problems. Black Supreme was just murdered inside of a Payless Shoe Store on Fulton Street. I didn't know the Bloods shopped at Payless." Justin bent down closer to his brother's ear so the other officer couldn't hear what he had to say. "If you're responsible for the girl and her grandmother's death, your ass and your whole crew is going down." Justin stood up and turned to the other officer. "Let 'em go," he said before walking out the door.

* * * * *

In an adjacent room from where Butter's interrogation took place, Spyda sat handcuffed while two plainclothes detectives took turns using his face as a punching bag.

"So, Spyda, you still don't have anything to say to us? You wanna still play like Mister It?" A short, stocky, black detective stood over Spyda as blood poured from Spyda's mouth.

"Man, fuck y'all! Y'all pigs can suck my dick."

SMACK!

Spyda fell out of the chair and onto the floor from the impact of the slap. The two detectives had been taking turns abusing him since taking him into custody. During the arrest, Spyda had spit on one of the detectives and that pissed them off, not to mention the loaded Tec-9 in his possession upon his arrest. The more Spyda spit and cursed at the officers, the more vicious the beatings got. When Detective Diekman walked into the room, Spyda was laying on the floor.

"What the fuck is going on in here?" Diekman asked his fellow detectives as he helped Spyda to his feet. "I see you have been making friends with the two detectives." Justin pulled out a rag from his back pocket. "Uncuff him," he ordered the detectives.

When they uncuffed Spyda, Justin passed him the rag to wipe the blood from his face. After he finished, Justin motioned for the officers to put the handcuffs back on him. Justin then pushed what appeared to be a Ziploc bag containing the Tec-9 towards Spyda. "Do you recognize this? Is this yours?" Justin asked as he pointed to the gun.

"Nah man, I never saw that gun before in my life," Spyda responded while spitting some remaining blood from his mouth.

"How can you say you never saw this gun before when the detectives took this off of your person when they arrested you?"

"Man, the police is the most corrupted muthafuckas I know. They must've planted that shit on me. That's what y'all do." Spyda turned and spat the blood from in his mouth on the floor at the feet of the short detective. Without warning, the officer swung. Spyda, not being able to block the blow because his hands were cuffed behind him, prepared for the blow.

SMACK!

Once again, Spyda hit the floor.

"Officer Barton! We're not here to batter the prisoner. Please, go take care of some paperwork and let me and Officer Kenneth take care of this." Justin handed the bag containing the gun to Barton as he exited the room.

"Bitch ass nigga! If I didn't have on these cuffs, it would be a different story!" Spyda screamed at Barton as he left the room.

"Spyda, would you like to press charges on Detective Barton?" Justin asked while helping Spyda back in his chair.

"Nah, I don't get down like that. I'm a firm believer in what goes around comes around. That faggot will get his."

"Spyda, I have known you since grade school; we both come from the same project. You know me, and you know you can talk to me. You and my brother have been going at each other's necks for a while now. When do you think it's time to put an end to all the madness? When one

76

of you is dead? Or when you make a mistake and kill one of them innocent kids who play in the playground? What y'all doing is senseless."

"Come on, Diekman, don't act like you down for the people. You're just as bad as your brothers. The only difference is that you're licensed to do what you're doing. The reason for what me and your snake-ass brother are going through is because of his jealousy. That's why my man Rashawn is dead now. Your family got the whole old side of the project brainwashed with that Blood shit. I'm just surprised you didn't follow in their footsteps. I know that must break their bitch-ass hearts."

"Spyda, you know I've always been my own man, but that's enough about me and my family. What about the girl and her grandmother that was killed? The word on the streets is that you hit up Rashawn to take over, and then hit up the girl because she saw you. And in the process, you killed the grandmother. The funny thing is I see why you would murder the girl and the grandmother because you know they could identify you. Whoever killed them was let in the house; they didn't enter by force. That tells me they knew and trusted the killers."

"Man, be for real. Everybody knows your brother killed them people, including my boys Rashawn, Chuck, and Hunt. I had mad love for Destiny and Ms. Hardy. But you shouldn't be questioning me. This shit stems deeper than me; this shit goes back to your family. Wasn't it your brothers that killed Destiny's father and mother about eight or nine years ago? Maybe your brother, or even you, was trying to finish the job. But y'all missed one." Spyda sat back and started laughing, knowing he had plucked a nerve.

Justin just looked at Spyda. He knew Spyda had a good point, which was one of the reasons he hated his family. Justin dreaded the day Summer found out that he was the brother of the men who were responsible for her parents' death.

"Listen, you shit head, I have nothing to do with what my family has done or is doing, so let that be the last time you put me in that category!" Justin stood up and looked at his partner. "Lock this piece of shit back up."

* * * * *

"Yo, Damu!" An unmarked police car pulled up in front of the game room where Butter and his crew hung out. The crew of young thugs all turned their heads in the direction of the car, preparing to make a run when they realized it was the police. "We got some info for you. They just killed y'all man Black Supreme. We think it was Spyda and his crew. Let Butter know we gave y'all that info. He knows where to send the money to." The detective on the passenger side rolled the window up as they pulled off.

Half Pint, a dwarf who stood 3'11", grew up on the new side, and was blooded in the early 90's under Butter's brothers, turned to Dice, one of Butter's top guns.

"You heard what them beast just said?"

"They said Spyda and them niggas just killed Black Supreme. Yo, let's get at them niggas now before they have a chance to talk about what they did to Blood. I know that's not how y'all Bloods in Brooklyn is letting niggas carry y'all." Gutter was one of the upstate Bloods that Butter brought to Brooklyn to put in some work for this war.

"Man, that shit might be a setup for us to get our heads knocked off," Dice responded as he passed Gutter the chief they were smoking.

"Nah, Dice, the Bloods had the 77th precinct on the payroll since the early days. Those niggas is Damu. It's the 71st we got to watch out for. That's where Butter's brother Justin works. It's personal with them because of Butter and his brother. All we need is for Butter to give the word and his ass is out."

As they all reflected on what the detectives from the 77th precinct just told them, Two-Guns Paul ran towards them.

"Yo, did y'all hear what happened?"

"What?" Half Pint asked, wanting to hear what he had to say.

"They locked up Butter, and them niggas from the old side killed Black Supreme on Fulton earlier." Two-Guns spoke in a heavy, out of breath voice.

"How you find this out?"

"That crackhead nigga PJ said he saw when they locked Butter up and his niece told him what happened to Black Supreme because she was on Fulton when the shooting happened. She saw Big Ruben and Justice run from the scene."

As everybody stood in shock, Dice's two-way went off. Dice looked at the number and quickly recognized it. He pulled out his cell and immediately called the number back.

"Yo, Butter, what's up? They just told me they locked you up."

"Yeah, Blood, that bitch-ass brother of mines questioning me about Rashawn and Destiny's murder. Yeah, that lil' bitch-ass nigga just on my dick because he wants to be me. Ya heard? But, yo, them fools from the old side killed Black Supreme!"

"Yeah, we know. The 77th came by and gave us that info and told us it was Spyda's crew. They also said you know where to send the check."

"Send some of the lil' homies to take care of the old side tonight, and I think it's time we send my bitch-ass brother a message about fucking with Blood. Meet me at the spot on Albany and Pacific."

"A'ight, Blood! One!" Dice hung up the phone and turned to the crew of killers. "That was Butter; he wants us to eat tonight."

"Yeah, yeah! Let me and Gutter handle that," Half Pint said with excitement.

"Nah, I need you and the crew to handle the store." Dice turned to Two-Guns and told him to snatch up two or three young homies to let them earn some stripes.

"A'ight, Blood!" Two-Guns Paul waved three of the lil' homies that was in the game room to come with him.

As they walked off, Gutter said, "Make sure we read about them niggas in the morning paper."

Dice jumped in his hoopty and pulled off to go pick up Butter.

* * * * *

After Cookie and Penny left, Summer laid back down. The weed she had smoked for the first time had given her a crazy headache and left her somewhat dazed, and not to mention, the realization that Cookie and Penny, her two best friends, had made a dramatic turn from being two polite, smart, and quiet people to two gangsta bitches who smoked weed and sniffed cocaine. All this change took place over the last three months.

They told Summer of the rumors spreading around about who murdered Destiny and Ms. Hardy. It was easy for Summer to believe Butter Bean and his crew was behind it, but what bugged her out was the fact that Spyda's name was also implemented. Her grandmother had actually took a liking to him, and just thinking about Spyda violating made Summer's stomach turn. Whoever was responsible had taken the only family she had away from her, and she swore on their lives she wouldn't rest until justice was served. Not by the police, but street justice.

The reality of the harsh world made her heart as cold as ice; and her lust for the blood of those who murdered her sister and grandmother was what fueled her desire to live. Not only did the deaths of Destiny and Ms. Hardy change Summer's life, but also Cookie's and Penny's, as well. The two of them agreed to help Summer in any form or fashion, and they agreed if the truth didn't surface soon on who was responsible, then both parties whose names were involved would have to answer for the deaths.

Cookie was fucking with this cat named Capone, Sha's brother. Capone introduced Cookie and Sha, who shared the same intention of finding out who was responsible for Rashawn's death. Sha and Cookie had become close since Sha's release from prison. When Cookie learned that Sha was fucking with Spyda and Butter at the same time, Cookie figured they could use Sha to their advantage.

Sha didn't have anything against Destiny. In fact, she never met her, but did find out Destiny was dating Rashawn while she was in jail. Still, that didn't change Sha's love for Rashawn and the hate she felt towards Butter and Spyda. Sha let Cookie in on her plans to get to the bottom of who set Rashawn up, and that she was going to kill whoever was responsible. Sha also told Cookie that was why she was playing both sides and that her brother was backing up her move. Rashawn was the one who had put her brother on, so he felt like he owed Rashawn that much. Cookie had called and introduced Sha to Summer over the phone, and they set a meeting for the next day. Sha was older than they were and wilder, but Summer had the determination and great hatred in her heart.

Summer was anxious about meeting Sha. Over the years, they had heard about Sha's street creditability and beauty. When Destiny first found out Sha was coming home, they thought they were going to have problems. The girls were actually scared of Sha, but Destiny was head over heels for Rashawn and under his spell. But now Destiny and Rashawn were dead, and Sha was willing to work with Summer to find out who killed them.

Summer laid back on the couch thinking about the days ahead, and before she knew it her eyes became heavy and she slipped into sleep.

* * * * *

"Grandma, do you think my mommy is going to be a big star?"

"Baby, your mother is already a big star. She'll always be a star to us no matter what."

"Grandma, I love my mommy, daddy, little sister, and you with all my heart."

"You suppose to, baby, and we love you just as much. We are family, and family is supposed to always love and protect one another till the day we die. You got to make sure that nothing ever happens to your little sister. Always

love her no matter what, even if y'all are mad at each other. There is no stronger bond than that of family."

"Grandma, do you have a sister?"

"Yeah, but my sister died a long time ago. She still lives in my heart and mind, though. So I live for the both of us."

"So your sister is here with us now?"

"Yes, baby, right here in our hearts, and she's watching over us right now."

"So she's like our guardian angel?"

"Yes, she is, and when I die, I'll be watching over y'all, as well."

"And you will always be right here in my heart."

"Awww, baby, that's sweet. Give Grandma a kiss."

BING BONG…BING BONG…

Summer jumped up from the couch and ran towards the front door. "Grandma, it's the door. It's probably Mommy and Daddy!"

"Summer, don't open that door!" Ms. Hardy got up and laid Destiny, who was asleep in her arms, on the couch as she walked behind Summer to open the door. Summer looked up at her grandmother with excitement in her eyes, hoping it was her parents.

"Yes, can I help you?" Ms. Hardy asked as she looked out the peephole and noticed two men dressed in suits standing in front of the door. One of the men pulled out his wallet, flashed a badge, and placed it in front of the peephole to show they were police officers.

"Summer, go have a seat on the couch." Ms. Hardy opened the door. As soon as the door opened, the two officers flashed their gold shields once more so Ms. Hardy could get a closer look.

"Hi, I'm Detective Brooks, and this is my partner Detective Tracy. Is this the home of Mr. & Mrs. Johnson?" the taller of the two asked.

"Yes, that's my daughter and her husband. Is everything alright? Are they hurt?" Ms. Hardy asked, sensing something wrong. She looked both detectives in their eyes and knew this visit wasn't good. Ms. Hardy could feel Summer standing at her side.

"Can we come in and speak to you?"

Just from the sound of the officer's voice, her stomach started turning and tears formed in the corners of her eyes. Ms. Hardy placed one hand over her mouth while she grabbed hold of Summer by her head. "Oh my God! What happened to my baby?"

Both detectives put their heads down, and once again, the taller of the two spoke in a firm but sympathetic voice. "Your daughter and son-in-law were both murdered outside of the club about an hour ago. We need you to come down and identify their bodies."

Ms. Hardy felt weak in the knees and felt like she was going to faint, when she realized Summer was standing next to her and had heard every word.

"Nooooo!" Summer screamed as she ran to the couch and tried to wake up her sister. Summer hugged her sister as she screamed for her mother and father. Each word the detective said hit Summer like a sharp pain, and she understood perfectly what they had said.

* * * * *

Summer jumped up, covered in sweat. Her head was killing her, and her mouth felt like she had drunk a whole glass of sand. This was the second time today she dreamed about the day her parents were murdered. She'd had these dreams frequently over the years, but never back to back on the same day. Summer felt like this was her parents' way of getting back at her for not protecting Destiny.

Summer looked around the living room and then at the clock. It was 2 a.m. After rising from the couch, she went into the bathroom to wash her face and brush her teeth to get the nasty taste out of her mouth. In the bathroom, she leaned over the sink and wet her face in an attempt to pull herself together. After wiping the water from her eyes, she looked at herself in the mirror. For the first time, Summer noticed how bad she looked. She had really let herself go.

"Fuck!" Summer banged her hand on the sink as she started crying profusely. She had promised herself that she wouldn't cry, but she could no longer hold it. She felt so alone, and the guilt and pain was unbearable. Summer tried to convince herself it wasn't her fault Destiny was murdered, but she was always taught Destiny was her responsibility since she was the oldest.

"Why?! Why did y'all have to leave me? I'm so alone and afraid. Why?!" Summer stared at herself once again in the mirror as she questioned her family for leaving her all alone. On top of that, her recent actions had her in a state of confusion. Yesterday, she left the institution, had sex with a man she hardly knew, and today, used drugs for the first time.

After about thirty minutes of contemplating the last couple of months of her life and feeling sorry for herself, the anger set in, and Summer washed her face, got dressed, and left out the house.

Chapter 6
Move The Crowd

Sha pulled up in front of the old side of the Pj's, where a group of Spyda's boys was all standing rolling dice. Two of the lookouts were the only ones who looked up from the dice game.

"Heads up," one of the lookouts said, not recognizing who was in the truck because of the dark tint on the windows. Bill Blast and Kevin both looked up, and Kevin walked over to the truck when he recognized who it was.

"Yo, what's up, Sha?" Kevin asked as he stuck his head in the window.

"Damn, Kevin, back your drunk ass up a little." Kevin was known for drinking his forty ounces of ole Gold, and when he got drunk, his ass stayed in a bitch's face. "They just locked Spyda up, and Big Ruben told me to come collect the money from you just in case Spyda needs it for bail."

"Word! For what and when?"

"I don't know…a couple of hours ago."

The whole crew wanted to get at Sha, but they knew she was faithful to Rashawn. Now that she was dealing with Spyda, they all wished they would have pushed up. Not only was Sha drop-dead gorgeous in the looks department and had a perfect ten body-wise, but she was also about her business in the streets.

"I have about thirteen at the down-low crib. Take Bill Blast with you to go get it." Kevin waved Bill Blast over. "Yo, they just locked up Spyda and he needs bail money. Take Sha to the crib and give her the money we have there."

"A'ight, son." Bill Blast was definitely down with being alone with Sha; he wanted to talk to her anyway.

Bill Blast was tight with Rashawn and didn't trust Spyda, but he kept that to himself for the time being because he knew Spyda had a lot of pull amongst the crew since he treated them better than Rashawn did. In return, they were loyal, but Bill Blast wasn't feeling the fact that Spyda took over and that his name was mentioned in setting Rashawn up. Bill Blast wasn't from the Pj's, but he and Rashawn became close during their stay on the ROC, Riker's Island.

Bill Blast jumped in the truck. "You know where the crib is at?" he asked while looking at Sha's thighs that were revealed through the high split in her dress. With Sha sitting with her legs open, Bill Blast's manhood started to stiffen.

"No, I never knew where the crib was located. Rashawn got that spot after I was locked up."

"It's on Dean and Underhill."

Sha turned the music back up and pulled off.

"Yo, Sha, you looking real good, girl. I don't know why you fucking with that nigga Spyda. You should have given a nigga like me some play. You know I've been feeling you for a while, even before Rashawn."

"Yeah, Blast, what brought all this on all of a sudden? You trying to push up on a sistah knowing I fuck with one of your boys?" Sha asked, trying to figure out Bill Blast's angle.

"Come on, Sha you know Rashawn was the only nigga I fucked with. The rest of these niggas is snakes and dick riders. I think these niggas set my man up. The only reason I'm still fucking with these cats is because I have a lot invested. On the real, I know you ain't feeling that nigga, either. I know how you felt about my man. That's why I never tried to push up on you. Plus, the other day, I saw you with that nigga Butter from the new side. So, I know you just using the nigga to get what you want. Fuck 'em! He's soft like that. Get whatever you can from the nigga."

"What?" Sha asked in a surprised tone. "You ain't never seen me with no Butter. Why would I be with that nigga knowing he was responsible for killing Rashawn?" Sha tried to deny being with Butter, while at the same time trying to figure out when Bill Blast could have seen them. She made it her business to be careful never to be seen with him.

"Come on, Sha, how long have you known me? You know how close me and Rashawn were. Do you think if I knew Butter was the one who murdered Rashawn I wouldn't have bodied that nigga already? Come on now. You don't have to play the roll with me. I can pick you out of a sea of many. I saw you one day when I was driving thru. You was in a cab talking to Butter. I never said nothing to that nigga Spyda, though, because for all I know, he might be the one who set my man up to take over. And these nigga worship him like he's God or something."

"So, Blast, you think Spyda had something to do with Rashawn's murder?"

"Come on, Sha, you ain't blind. Who's benefiting from his death the most? Spyda was Rashawn's 'yes man' and now he's that dude."

"I don't know, Blast. Do you have proof?"

"Listen, just forget it. Fuck that nigga. He knows I'm not feeling him. In the long run, everything is gonna come to light. That's enough about that soft nigga. I know you ain't feeling that nigga like that. You're too raw for him. What's up with me and you?"

"Come on, Blast you know I don't get down like that." As Sha drove, she tried to figure out what was Bill Blast trying to tell her and why. Why wasn't he scared she would go back and tell Spyda what he was saying to her? Did he really know something, and what was he trying to tell her? "Blast, is there something you're trying to tell me or that you want me to know?"

"Nah, it's nothing. When the time comes everything will be revealed. What I'm really trying to say is what's up with me and you swinging sometime? We both grown folk and we can enjoy each other's company sometime."

Sha drove in deep thought for a minute while Bill Blast kept trying to push up on her. Sha thought about the cards that were dealt to her. To get at whoever was responsible for killing Rashawn, she was willing to play the game.

"So if I gave you a piece, what's in it for me? You know a sistah got to get hers. And you know money is not an object to me, so your money means nothing."

"Word, talk to me. What's up?"

"Like you said, in due time. Just remember if I did give you a piece, you owe me, and when the time comes, I want you to show me some love."

"Listen, baby girl, I'm yours."

"Blast, whatever we do gots to be between just you and me."

"Come on, ma, I'ma a grown man. You think I'ma kiss and tell?" Bill Blast pointed to a gray apartment building, and Sha pulled the Range in front and parked. "You coming up?" Bill Blast asked.

"Only if you don't put my business out in the streets, because if you do, I'ma have to body you."

Bill Blast laughed, but Sha didn't crack a smile. She knew Bill Blast knew who was responsible for Rashawn's murder; he was just scared to let it be known. She reached over, removed her gun from the glove compartment, and put it in her bag.

"Damn, boo, you rolling with Blast. You don't need that."

"Shiiit! I told you if you kiss and tell, I'ma kill that ass."

Sha smiled as she got out of the truck and followed Bill Blast into the building. Sha figured if Bill Blast was willing to go behind Spyda's back and push up on her, knowing that Spyda would have him killed, she knew he knew something and therefore could use him to her advantage. Sha had no intentions on giving Bill Blast the coochie, but she would let him suck on the cat for about thirty minutes and let him get a taste of heaven just to get him open. She could go for her pussy being eaten right now anyway. Lately, she enjoyed getting her pussy serviced by a strong tongue more than a hard dick. Therefore, she was willing to let him do her so she could get pleased and get what she wanted, also.

* * * * *

"Yo, come in! The door is open," Butter screamed.

As soon as Dice entered the crib, he froze. "Yo, Butter, what the fuck?"

Butter was sitting on the couch smoking a blunt and getting his head blown.

"Nigga, you act like you never seen a nigga getting his helmet polished. Dice, I want you to send some of the young homies to go tighten up my brother. He's getting too big for his britches. He's a little too loose lately. He acts like he don't remember that Blood protected his ass all these years."

Butter paused as Passion took his entire shaft down her throat. Butter inhaled the weed smoke, chiefing on a blunt laced with dust. Passion, who just turned sixteen, leaned over and pressed her face deeply between his legs. Butter used Passion to transport his drugs and money from spot to spot. He had taught her how to give head, but he never had sex with her and made sure nobody else did. She was to save herself for him and him alone.

As she slid his manhood in and out of her mouth, making a lot of wet sounds, Dice tried to ignore it, but actually his dick was getting hard from the sound and the act. He had wanted to fuck Passion's young ass, but knew Butter wasn't having that. Passion wore one of Butter's t-shirts with nothing on underneath. The shirt was riding above her hips, allowing Dice to see every inch of her thickness. She had the perfect apple bottom.

"Yo, Butter, I'ma go in the back. Holla at me when you finish." Dice couldn't take it. Standing there while she handled Butter like the trooper she was had him going crazy. He wanted to take the pussy, so he had to get away.

Butter lay back with the blunt in his mouth and both hands on her head. Grabbing a handful of her hair to guide her jaws as she grunted and gagged, Butter tried to shove all of his manhood down her throat. He closed his eyes and pushed Passion's head down his shaft, forcing her to take more of his manhood into her mouth as he came. Passion made it her business to not spill one drop of his cum she swallowed. She enjoyed pleasing Butter orally. In return, he gave her whatever she wanted and protected her. Since being with Butter, she was well respected and the flyest dressed in school with all the latest fashions…and not with urban wear, but shit like Gucci, Dolce & Gabbana, and other shit she could hardly pronounce. The fact that she was still a virgin made her a top choice.

Passion stood up. "Daddy, did you enjoy yourself?"

"Sure did, baby girl. I was at the point of no return. You almost made me break my promise. I was close to telling you to bend over or ride me so I could handle that sweet thang for you."

"Daddy, you know you can whenever you're ready. This is all for you and nobody else."

"Yeah, I know. That's why I'm waiting until the time is right."

"Daddy, I'm ready now, and I'm not giving myself to no one else. Nobody make me feel the way you make me feel just from being around you." Passion leaned over and started sucking on Butter's neck.

"Don't worry, baby girl, when it happens, it will be magic. I just want you to make sure that's what you want, because once you lose your virginity, you can't get it back. I want it to be special for the both of us, and not just because you feel like you owe me, but because of love."

With each word Butter spoke, he stroked her young mind and caused her to fall more in love with him, which was his goal. After a few minutes, Butter got up and walked to the back where Dice was watching Sport's Center on ESPN.

"Damn, Blood, Passion is a bad girl. I see why you don't even let niggas say nothing to her. And you still didn't hit them young draws yet? I find that shit hard to believe. Shorty is a dime."

"Nah, Scooby, I didn't hit it yet. I want her to fiend a lil' bit, but when the time is right and I feel she's ready to commit her life to me, then and only then will I bless her. By then, she'll be ready to die for me." Butter inhaled the weed and dust blunt he had taken from behind his ear and re-lit, then passed it to Dice.

"Man, Butter, you crazy. Shorty will do anything for you *now*. She don't even look at other niggas. I done seen plenty of niggas trying to holla at shorty, and she just keep it moving."

"I know, dog, but let a pimp walk these dogs, Blood. If a bitch ain't ready to lay her life down for a nigga or ready to kill for a nigga, the bitch ain't worth the time, ya heard. Just because a bitch can suck a good dick and the pussy is half-ass good, don't mean she's the one. The loyalty got to be first. I can get my dick sucked from these nickel and dime ass bitches. They come a dime a dozen. But a bitch that has something to offer more than her sex is what I'm trying to shape and mold. A perfect bitch to me is made. Not some already made hoe who thinks she knows something and you can't tell her nothing. And that there, Blood, is what I'm doing to my good girl in there...molding her."

"I feel you, Blood. What's up with Sha? She's still fucking with that lame nigga Spyda."

"Yeah, you see, Sha is that type of girl you use for what you want. She's a dime, but poison to the core. She can't be trusted as far as you can throw her. She'll stab you in the back, and a weak nigga, she'll make a girl out of him every time. That's why I fuck with her because she's about her business. We ain't going to have to worry about them niggas, 'cause we'll be able to get to them through her. So, we got to keep her close. She's vicious, a cold-blooded killer, not to mention we can kill two birds with one stone. Through her, we can get close to her brother, gain his trust, and move on him when he least expects it."

"Yeah, he's eating real good, too. I heard he be fucking with them Crabs over in Crown Heights."

"Yeah, but the nigga is neutral."

"Come on, Blood, you know how that shit go. I feel a nigga is guilty by association."

"You know I feel you, but we'll talk about that another time. Right now, it's about sending my punk ass brother a message. I think he needs an eye opener. I don't want them to kill him, just rough him up a little. And what about the other detail involving Black Supreme? Did you send some of the soldiers to give the old side a makeover? I think if we paint them muthafuckas red, it would be a good look. Those niggas got to answer for what they did to Black Supreme."

"Yeah, you know all that's being taken care of. I sent Two-Guns Paul and a couple of the homies to put that work in. You know them lil' niggas was dying to put some work in on them fools. Yo, Dog, what happened when the beast snatched you up?"

"My bitch ass brother's questioning a nigga about them murders a couple of months ago. Somebody is trying to point the finger at us. Yo, the nigga even asked me if I killed Hunt and Chuck. Did y'all get rid of them burners?"

"Yeah, me and Black Supreme got rid of them joints that night."

"What's poppin' at the spot? They should be ready for some more work, right?"

"I left Half Pint and Gutter there. They should be ready for some more. When I left, they only had about half a brick left, and it's the first of the month. Shit was moving."

Butter went into the dresser and pulled out a brown paper bag. "Yo, Passion, come here for a minute." Before Butter could turn around Passion was standing in the doorway. Dice looked up and stared at Passion's nipples, which were poking out from beneath her t-shirt with no bra on.

"What's up, daddy?" Passion asked while smiling at Dice.

"Take this to the store, collect the money, and then stop at the weed gate and cop twenty bags of that crazy Eddie and a half ounce of that sticky." Butter passed Passion the shopping bag with the drugs in it, and then pulled out a mitt and peeled off five crispy hundred dollar bills. After handing her the money, he passed her the keys to his CLK. "Do you have your driver's permit with you?"

"Daddy, you know I have my license now."

"Oh a'ight, that's even better. Don't be out there fucking around. Do what you have to do and get back here."

"A'ight, daddy." Passion kissed Butter before turning to leave the room to get dressed. Dice watched as she walked away. He was really feeling Passion, and wished she wasn't with Butter because he knew Butter was only going to use and abuse her. And to him, Passion deserved better.

"Yo, Butter, who do you want me to send at Justin?"

"Any of the lil' homies from upstate. Just make sure they know not to kill him."

"You got it, boss. I'm 'bout to be out. I'll call you when shit goes down."

"One!"

As soon as Dice left out the house and Passion was gone, Butter called Sha. Passion had put Butter in the mood for some of Sha's loving.

* * * * *

As soon as Sha collected all of the money from Bill Blast and let him eat her pussy for about half an hour, she left. She told him that she would get back with him later that night so they could finish what they started. Bill Blast told Sha that he thought Spyda was the one who set Rashawn up, and that he was willing to kill Spyda when the time was right. Sha convinced Bill Blast the only reason she was dealing with Spyda was to find out who killed Rashawn, and if what he was saying was true, then Spyda had to die. As Sha climbed into her truck, her cell phone went off. She looked at the number, but didn't answer. Once it stopped ringing, Sha called Big Ruben.

"Ruben, what happened with Spyda? Did they give him a bail?"

"We're on our way to Queens right now. We was sidetracked for a minute and had to change rides. We ran into one of them niggas and had to take care of something, but we're headed that way now."

96

"Well, I collected thirteen from Kevin and Bill Blast. I'm headed for the crib. When you find something out, call me."

"A'ight, Sha. Thanks."

After Sha hung her phone up, it started ringing again. Recognizing the number on the caller ID, she answered it. It was the same number that called before she called Big Ruben. "Hello."

"Hey, boo, what's really good?"

"Oh hey, Butter, what 'cha doing?"

"Thinking about hitting them draws. What's up?"

"You know the police locked that nigga Spyda up."

"Word! That's why them muthafuckas snatched me up today asking about them murders. That bitch nigga must have told them that I killed Rashawn and them other people. That snake muthafucka. Them niggas murdered my lil' man Black Supreme today."

"Oh no!" The first thing that came to Sha's mind was what Big Ruben just told her about them being sidetracked and having to change cars. "Butter, do y'all know who did it?"

"Yeah, that nigga Big Ruben and Justice."

"Butter, listen, I'm about to meet up with Big Ruben in a few. I'm just waiting for him to call me back so they can bail out Spyda. What do you want to do?"

"Yeah!" Butter yelled. "That's why I'm feeling you, boo. You think like I think. We can get that nigga Spyda, too?"

"Nah, Butter we can't get to Spyda right now...not in front of the courts. We'll have to get him another time. Don't worry about Spyda right now. I have something else planned for his snake ass. You kill off his strength and muscle, he don't have nothing. You know he's a pussy without his guns, and Big Ruben and Lil Just are his guns. So, you get Ruben and Justice for now."

"Yo, Sha, I love you. Will you marry me?"

"Nigga, please, so I can kill your ass over your lil' sex slave, Passion?"

"What you talking about? Passion is just my runner."

"Come on, Butter, I've been doing this too long. Just be ready when I call you to let you know where to meet me."

"A'ight, ma. One!"

CLICK...

Chapter 7
The Payback Is Always Sweeter

Summer sat at the bar and ordered a Long Island Ice Tea. The bar was crowded with a lot of old men and trick-ass bitches trying to trick the men out of their money. The atmosphere was grimy, but this was what Summer wanted to be around to clear her head and think. The guilt of Destiny and Ms. Hardy's deaths was weighing heavy on her mind. Summer put the blame on herself and felt as if she didn't keep her promise of always protecting her little sister. For her pain and grief, something had to give and soon.

Spyda and Butter's names were implemented in the murders, so she decided they would have to both pay for her sister's death regardless of who actually did it. She was willing to put her life on the line to kill Butter, Spyda, and whoever else got in her way.

Although she was feeling Justin, he was the police and wanted the people who were responsible put in jail, whereas Summer wanted them dead…an eye for an eye. And she wouldn't rest until it was done. Summer knew Cookie and Penny were willing to help her, but she felt it was something she had to do on her own.

Summer smiled at the bartender as he poured her drink in front of her. "Thank you." As Summer lifted her drink to her mouth, she felt somebody standing behind her.

"Excuse me, but is this chair taken?" Summer turned around to answer the person, and a short, light-skinned dude with wavy hair and a mouth full of platinum and diamonds blinded her when he smiled. He looked familiar, but she couldn't place a name to the face.

"No, no one is sitting here. The seat is open," Summer answered as she quickly turned her attention back to her thoughts and drink.

"Can I buy you another drink, ma? Perhaps we can share a bottle of Cristal?" The dude sat next to Summer and motioned for the bartender.

"Sure, I would love to join you for a drink."

The dude extended his hand. "My name is Justice. Are you from around here, because you look real familiar?"

When Justice said his name, Summer looked at him again and then it registered where she recognized him from. Justice was Spyda's right-hand man. He didn't recognize her probably because she had lost a lot of weight while in the hospital and her once long, silky hair was now dreads. This was a good thing because she could make her move and this fool wouldn't even know it was coming. Summer knew if Spyda had anything to do with the murder of her family, Justice was down with it, and for that, he would have to pay, also. Even if he wasn't down with it, fuck it. He was guilty by association.

"No, I'm not from around here, but I've had a lot of people say that I look familiar or like somebody they know. You know they say everybody has a twin out here in the world." Summer shook Justice's hand and said, "Hi, my name is Martha, and I'm from Queens."

"So, Martha, what are you doing in a place like this all alone in Brooklyn?" The bartender finally walked over to Justice. "Yo, let me get a bottle of Cristal and two glasses for me and the young lady." Justice turned his attention back to Summer and looked her in the eyes as he waited for her answer to his question.

"Well, I just wanted to get away from my area for awhile. I recently got out of an abusive relationship, and the people out there are always in other people's business. So, I chose to come to Brooklyn to get my drink on and stopped at the first bar I noticed. I guess I was sick of being cooped up in the house. I felt it was time for me to live my life like Mary J Blige says, 'with no more drama.' So, I decided to come have some drinks and enjoy myself."

"Um, I see. Are you enjoying yourself yet?"

"Well, I just got here about five minutes before you walked up."

"Well, Martha, what do you have in mind for fun and enjoyment?"

"I don't know. I'm new to this bar thing. It's been so long since I've been around other men I don't know how to act. My old boyfriend was real jealous. I wasn't allowed to be around other men. So I basically don't know how to have a good time. I was hoping to meet somebody that could show me."

"Damn, ma, you had it bad. Somebody as pretty as you should never be locked down and abused, nor be denied enjoying yourself. A man should be willing to give a jewel like you the world. I know you got men waiting in line to be with you."

Summer smiled. "You have no idea. You don't know how far away from the truth that is." The bartender came back with the bottle of Cristal and two glasses and poured their drinks. "Mmmm! I see you're a big baller, shot caller."

"Nah, ma, I just like the finer things in life and only the best for someone as special as you."

"I guess some of us have it like that."

"You can have it like that, too, if you roll with the right people." Justice looked into Summer's eyes as he thought about fucking the shit out of this slim goody. "So, Martha, what's your plan for the rest of the night?"

"I don't know. I was hoping a baller like you could tell me." Summer gave a provocative stare as she sipped her drink.

"Maybe you and I can break this camp and do our own thing."

"I would like to, but I don't know. It's kinda hard for me to be with another man right now."

Summer looked Justice in the eyes and then put her head down. She knew how to play on his intelligence. Justice was thinking with his dick and Summer knew this, so the harder she played to get, the more he would want her. That was just how men were. She banked on him being persistent.

"Come on, ma, let that no-good nigga go. Don't let him dictate your life no more. Remember Mary's words… 'No more drama.' Let me show you a good time, even if it's just for tonight."

"You're right, Justice. It's just so hard for me to let go. After loving and trusting a man who then throws your heart away, you become scorned."

Lil' Justice poured Summer another glass of the expensive bubbly. "I feel you, ma. That's why I want to at least take your mind away for awhile."

"Mmmm! That sure sounds good." As she sipped her Cristal, Summer once again gave Justice a look that said she was willing to do whatever he wanted to do. "You sure know how to make a sistah feel comfortable. What 'cha trying to do? Sweep me off of my feet?!"

"Is it working?"

"Maybe."

"Martha, do you like to chief?"

"Chief? What's that?"

Lil' Justice laughed at Summer's lack of understanding slang. "Puff weed!"

"Oh, do I smoke?" She giggled. "That's the new term for smoking weed now? Believe it or not, today was the first time I ever smoked weed or drank liquor."

"Damn! You're still wet behind the ears, huh?" Justice figured if he could get her to puff some of the chronic he had copped from the dread off the avenue, she would be an easy fuck.

"I don't know about smoking weed with strangers. You might try to put something in the weed to make me have sex with you." Summer smiled as she finished her drink and licked her lips, causing Justice's manhood to stand at attention,

Damn! I got something she can lick, Justice thought. "Come on, ma, I hope a nigga don't never have to be that desperate to give a shorty some type of date rape drug to have sex with them. I'm not that hard up."

"Maybe you won't, but how do I know that? I just met you at a bar."

"Ma, I guess life is full of chances. You got to be willing to chance life sometimes, or you might miss the chance of a lifetime." Justice refilled Summer's glass.

"What 'cha trying to do? Get a sistah drunk?"

"Nah, but I am trying to convince you to be with me for the rest of the night. I don't wanna be alone tonight, either. So maybe we can help each other out with our problems. Do I look like some type of deranged psycho?"

"No, but they usually don't look the part. They usually look like the guy next door."

"Yeah, but I don't look like the guy next door, do I? I promise I won't try nothing."

Summer leaned over and whispered in Justice's ear as she rubbed up his thigh. "I hope so because I usually don't do this, but there is something about you that I'm attracted to. And the fact that you only get to live once, I'm willing to give you a chance. Not to mention this champagne has a sister feeling horny."

"That's what I'm talking about, ma. Let's break this camp and live life to the fullest." Justice waved for the bartender, ordered another bottle of Cristal, and paid for everything. As Justice walked behind Summer, he pictured himself digging her back out, fucking the shit out of her all night. However, all that was on Summer's mind were the images of her sister's and grandmother's slain bodies.

* * * * *

After Big Ruben dropped Justice off at the bar and changed cars, he headed for Queens to meet up with Linda. When he walked into the house, Linda was on the phone with Spyda.

"Here, he wants to speak to you." Linda handed Big Ruben the phone. As soon as he took the phone, Linda dropped to her knees, unzipped his pants, and started giving him head while he was on the phone with Spyda. When Linda found out Spyda was fucking Sha, she pushed up on

Big Ruben one day, and they had been fucking behind Spyda's back ever since.

"Yo!" Big Ruben said as he tried to push Linda from his manhood, but she wouldn't let go.

"Yo, Ruben, my bail is twenty-five with a bail bondsman. Go see that nigga Truman. Linda got the number, and she should have fifteen in the house."

BigRuben strained not to grunt from the feeling of pleasure Linda was giving him. He felt guilty for fucking his man's girl, and had tried to break it off with her, but she knew how to get to a nigga. Not to mention, she had the best jaws in Brooklyn.

"A'ight, I have to go catch up with Sha. I had her collect the money we had out in the streets from Kevin and Bill Blast. I'ma send her." Big Ruben shut his eyes tight, fighting to suppress his moans. He covered the phone's mouthpiece, hoping Spyda didn't hear the slurping sound. It was as if Linda wanted Spyda to know they were fucking.

"Yo, Ruben, I heard about Black Supreme."

"Yeah, you know that was my work. I caught the nigga slipping."

"A'ight, Ruben, I'll build with you later."

"I'm on my way now to take care of that. You'll be out of there by tonight."

"A'ight. One!"

"One!"

CLICK...

As soon as Big Ruben hung the phone up, he pulled off his pants, turned Linda around, and fucked her on the couch.

* * * * *

After Spyda hung up, the C.O. escorted him back to the holding pen. The judge had granted him bail and now he was just waiting for Sha to come get him. Upon his release, he planned to take her to the hotel across the street from the court house and fuck her brains out to show his appreciation. When Spyda entered back into the holding cell, the C.O. had placed another inmate in the cell with him while he was on the phone. The dude was stretched out on the bench. Spyda walked up and tapped him on the leg.

"Yo, fam, could you slide down a little so I can sit with you?"

The dude looked up and saw Spyda's swollen lip from where the police had punished him and figured Spyda for a pussy. This made the dude respond with disrespect. "Yo, Blood!" the dude said, letting it be known that he was Blood. "Sit on the floor before I do something to that ass worse than you already got." The dude lay back down after speaking, like he was the shit.

"What?!" Spyda couldn't believe the lil' nigga tried to get out on him. Spyda knew he was about to get bailed out, so he didn't wanna flip on him.

"Yo, nigga, you heard what the fuck I sai..."

Before the dude could finish what he was saying, Spyda pulled him off the bench by his leg, causing him to hit the floor face first. Spyda then stomped and rained on the dude's head.

"C.O! Yo, C.O.!" the dude screamed as he tried his best to cover up from Spyda's assault. It seemed like about twenty minutes before Spyda heard the cell cracking and the C.O.'s came running in, snatching him off of the dude and dragging the dude out of the holding cell.

* * * * *

Justin got out, locked the car door behind him, and set his alarm. He had a long day and no leads on numerous murder cases yet. Justin inhaled the night's air as he walked towards his house, which was still in the hood. Before coming home, he stopped by Summer's but received no answer. He even called and the phone just rang. He wanted to get in the house to see if she had left a message on his answering machine. This case was stressing him, and the fact that his brother was probably in some way involved made it just that crazier. Not to mention, he was falling in love with Summer and taking this case a little too personal. He knew a relationship with her wouldn't work once she found out he was the brother to the people who were responsible for murdering her parents and maybe her sister and grandmother, as well.

As Justin reached his front gate and pulled out his house keys, a stray cat jumped out of the garbage can. "Oh shit!" Justin jumped as the cat startled him. "Stupid cat…stay out the damn garbage can!" Justin kicked at the cat, missing him by a mile as the cat ran off.

"Yo, Diekman!"

As soon as Justin tried to turn to see who had called his name, he was struck by an object.

CRACK!!!

Justin was barely able to throw his arm up to block the blow from hitting him in the head and face. The two assailants continued to swing bats at Justin's head, knocking him to the ground. As the impact of hitting the ground knocked the air out of him, the two charged towards him once again with their bats raised in the striking position. Without hesitation, Justin reached for the revolver he had in his ankle holster and fired! Dropping both assailants, Justin jumped up from off the ground, still pointing his gun at the two men whose faces were covered with red bandanas. Justin's whole left side was numb, including his left arm, which he knew was broken. Justin kicked the bats away from the men who were laying on the ground moaning and grunting in pain from the hot ones Justin had pumped in them. After radioing into the station, Justin sat down on his stoop and waited for the police to arrive. He knew exactly who had sent them.

* * * * *

Big Ruben called Sha back as soon as he left Linda's house.

"Yo, Sha, Spyda's bail is twenty-five with a bailbonds man. Spyda wants you to go see him. I collected fifteen from Linda's house. Where are you? Do you want me to meet you at your house?" Big Ruben sat in his car fixing his clothes.

"I'm at my brother's house right now, so if you can, meet me on Macon and Patchen in about a half. You'll see me parked out front."

"A'ight, Sha, I'm on my way."

CLICK...

Big Ruben thought about Linda. He knew it was time for him to stop fucking with her because she was getting too reckless. It was as if she wanted Spyda to know he was fucking her because she wanted to get back at Spyda for fucking with Sha. But Big Ruben couldn't have that because Spyda was his man and too much was at stake to have to kill his man over some pussy. "But goddamn that pussy is good, and the head is out of this world!" he said to himself as he pulled off. Big Ruben flipped open his cell and dialed Justice's number.

* * * * *

Butter Bean lay in the bed waiting for Sha to call back with the time and place where she was meeting up with Big Ruben. Big Ruben was Spyda's main strength, and if he got him and Justice, all Spyda had were those bitch-ass niggas Kevin and Bill Blast. The rest of them lil' niggas would run with whoever was in power. Butter felt if he took the heads, the body would fall, especially with them being divided like they were. A lot of them niggas from the old side that was close to Rashawn felt Spyda snaked him, and the only reason they were still with him was because they were scared of Big Ruben and Justice. So Butter knew if he could get them out the way, he could take over the project.

He would leave Spyda to Sha. Then, they could concentrate on moving on Sha's brother, Capone. Butter planned on having his crew on top by the end of the year. His only problem outside of the street beef was his brother, Detective Justin Diekman. After tonight, though, Justin should get the message that even he could get it if he got in the Blood's way. Butter smiled to himself as his cell phone went off. Jumping out of the bed, he snatched the phone off his dresser.

"Yo!"

"Butter, it's Sha. I'm meeting Ruben in thirty minutes on Macon and Patchen."

"How many people is he bringing with him?"

"I don't know, but the last time I spoke to him he had Justice with him. I don't know if Justice was still with him just now, though."

"Do you know what kind of car he's driving?"

"Nah, but listen, y'all can't make a move until I get the bail money from him. Y'all will see me, and when I pull off, then y'all make y'all move."

"Yo, good looking out, Sha. I'ma get that nigga for my man. Don't feel bad for that nigga. You know Spyda used him to hit Rashawn. He was the only one of them niggas out that crew that had the heart to do that type of shit."

"Come on, Butter, if I was worried, I wouldn't have told you. But I want to get that nigga Spyda myself."

"Yo, Sha, we can get that nigga Spyda tonight, as well. He'll never be expecting us to move on him as soon as he gets bailed out."

"Nah, Butter, it's not right. I'ma have his own people snake."

"I hope so, and it's not the end of all this shit tonight."

"Come on, Butter, don't even try to get at that nigga yet...in due time. No time to argue about this right now. I'm on my way to Macon as we speak."

"A'ight, I'm on top of it. One!"

CLICK...

As soon as Butter hung up the phone from Sha, he called Dice.

"Hello."

"Yo, Dice, did you send Two-Guns and the lil' homies to hit up the old side yet?"

"Yeah, but nobody was out there. I'ma send them back around there in about a hour. I also sent the lil' homies at Diekman, but they haven't got back at me yet."

"Yo, it's going down. I'ma come pick up Two-Guns Paul and two of the homies. Tell them to be downstairs right now and to have their heat ready. I'm on my way."

"A'ight, dog. One!"

CLICK...

Chapter 8
Don't Trust Nobody

Justice pulled into the driveway of one of the newly remodeled homes on the corner of Dekalb and Broadway.

"Who lives here?" Summer asked.

"This is my crib. I rent the downstairs basement apartment. Come on, snatch up the bottle of Cristal." Justice exited the car and walked to his entrance to the basement. Summer snatched up the bottle and followed closely behind him. Her mind was racing a hundred miles per second, her palms were sweaty, and tears started forming in the corner of her eyes as she pictured her sister and grandmother's slain bodies.

Lil' Justice turned around and looked at her. "Ma, you alright? You look a little worried," he asked, noticing the look on Summer's face.

"I'm alright, just a little nervous. I told you that I haven't done this before and that it's been a while since I've been with a man other than my ex."

"Ma, don't worry, I'ma take care of you."

After Justice opened the door to his apartment, they entered and walked down a flight of stairs. As soon as he turned on the lights in the living room, Summer made her move. Without hesitation, she swung the bottle with all her might, smashing it across the back of Justice's head and knocking him to the floor. Summer then jumped on top of him, and with the jagged parts of the broken bottle, she slit Lil' Justice's throat from one side to the other.

"This is for my sister and grandmother, BITCH!"

Killing Justice immediately, Summer collected most of the pieces of broken glass and carefully wiped her fingerprints from them. Afterwards, she went into Justice's pocket and took every dime he had plus the 9mm stashed in his waist. Feeling somewhat satisfied, she left out the house like a thief in the night.

* * * * *

Sha left her brother's house and drove to Macon, where she parked in front of the park. The reason she told Big Ruben to meet her on Macon and Patchen was because of the school and park, which were closed at nighttime, so the block was somewhat deserted besides the crackheads that didn't give a fuck about nothing expect where their next rock was coming from. Sha spotted two shorties standing in the dark off in the cut when she entered the block. Five minutes after she parked, she noticed Big Ruben pulling up behind her. She couldn't tell from her rearview mirror if he was alone or not. Big Ruben got out of the car, walked to her truck, and jumped in.

"Yo, what's up, Sha?"

"Hey, Ruben, I'm tired as hell. Y'all got a sistah running around like a chicken with her head cut off."

"Come on, ma, you know your man Spyda is going to take care of you tonight for your troubles."

"He better," Sha said sarcastically.

"I feel you, but here's the address to the bailbonds man. He's waiting for you. The money is in this bag, fifteen thousand." Big Ruben passed Sha the piece of paper and sat the bag of money on the floor of her truck. "You have to go and meet the dude right now because he's waiting for you. They have until eleven o'clock tonight to bail him out, or we'll have to wait until tomorrow, and it's already 10:15. So, you got to move fast."

"A'ight, I'm headed that way as soon as you get out." Sha noticed the two young cats that were in the cut starting to walk towards them. They couldn't have been any older than fifteen or sixteen years old. They both had their hoodies over their head. Big Ruben didn't pay the two boys any mind as he got out of the truck and told Sha to tell Spyda to call him when he got out. Big Ruben wasn't on point, because if he was, he would have noticed the two young boys walking towards the truck had red bandanas hanging from the right sides of their pants. Sha hurried up, started her truck, and pulled off. As she turned the corner, she noticed from her rearview mirror the two approaching Big Ruben before he reached his car.

* * * * *

After the doctors put a cast on Justin's arm, he walked into the hallway where his partner Detective Kenneth was waiting.

"How's your arm?"

"Broken in two places, my wrist and forearm."

"Damn, pretty nasty breaks."

"What's the condition of the two kids I shot?"

"They'll live, but they're not talking. Do you have any idea who sent them after you?"

"Yeah, of course I do. I know just who sent those little punks after me because he was too scared to do it himself." Justin put his jacket on over his shoulders.

"You know, the lieutenant wants to see us as soon as you get out of the hospital."

"Yeah, well, I have a previous engagement. I'll get around to him tomorrow. Right now, I have family issues to deal with." Justin looked at his cast and smiled.

"Do you want me to go with you?"

"Nah, I'm alright. I got this." Justin walked off, leaving Kenneth standing in the hallway of the hospital. Before he walked out the door, he turned around. "Oh yeah, Ken, take a cab home, 'cause I need your car." Justin turned and walked out the door.

* * * * *

Half Pint and Gutter both had shorties in the back of the game room while Pusher Man was up front dealing with the customers. They had weed and cocaine pumping out of the game room. Half Pint had his shorty bent over in the corner of the room giving him the mean head, while Gutter struggled with his shorty. She wasn't trying to hear what Gutter was talking about. She was playing on some hard-to-get time.

"Yo, ma, what's the deal? You not feeling a nigga or something? You done smoked up all a nigga's weed, and now you're on some funny time." Gutter struggled and tugged at the girl's belt as she continued to push his hands away.

"Stop! It's not that I'm not feeling you; I'm just not like that. I just met you. What, am I supposed to be willing just to drop my draws to you because we smoked a blunt together? I don't think so."

"Damn, ma, look at your girl." Gutter pointed to her friend who was bent down on her knees giving Half Pint the jaws of death. "She's with it, so what's your problem?"

"That's her; she gets down like that, not me. Go over there to her. Maybe she'll do both of y'all."

"You know what, bitch?! Maybe you right. Get the fuck out before I put my foot up your ass." As soon as Gutter started to walk over to where Half Pint and his shorty were, he heard a big crashing sound coming from the front of the store.

"Oh shit! What the fuck was that?" Half Pint jumped up with his manhood swinging. As they all turned around, the back door flew open.

"Freeze! Police!"

*   *   *   *   *

Once Butter dropped Two-Guns Paul and Razor off on Macon, he headed for the game room. He wanted to check up on Gutter and Half Pint while waiting for the outcome of the Big Ruben situation. When Butter turned on the block of the game room, he witnessed about ten to fifteen police rushing into his spot.

"What the fuck!" Butter immediately picked up his phone to call Dice as he kept driving by.

"Hello."

"Dice, the police is running up in the spot right now."

"What? Say word!"

"Son, I just drove by and saw around twenty police running up in my shit."

116

"Yo, I'm on my way now."

"Nah, stay at the crib and wait to see if anybody calls. Have you heard from the lil' homies yet?"

"Nah, not yet. What precinct was it?"

"Man, you already know it was the 71st precinct. My muthafuckin' brother is behind this shit. I hope the lil' homies didn't fuck up. Do you think the lil' homies would have talked if they got knocked?"

"Nah, they know the penalty is death to speak on Blood affairs to the police. They wouldn't jeopardize their families like that. Besides, their whole family is Blood.'

"Ya, Blood, I hope so, because something ain't right. I'm headed to the crib. Meet me there."

"A'ight, Damu. One!"

CLICK...

After Butter hung up, he called Passion and told her to meet him at the crib because he had something for her to do.

"Yo, I hope these lil' niggas didn't go at my brother half-stepping and got themselves killed fucking with him. Damn!" Butter thought as he headed to the crib.

*   *   *   *   *

"Penny, this is me. Have you spoke to Summer since we left her crib?"

"This is me, who?" Penny asked, still sounding half sleep.

"Bitch, who else did you leave Summer's house with earlier? Girl, get your ass up!" Cookie screamed into the phone.

"Cookie, why the hell is you yelling? I'm sick as a dog. I came home and crashed out. Nah, I haven't spoken to her. Why? What's wrong?"

"Nothing, I was just trying to get in touch with her because I was about to go to her house. I left my keys to her house on her dresser and wanted to make sure she was there before I go all the way over there and she's not there. I've been trying to reach her for the last hour. I'm at Capone's house, but he left. You know how that nigga stay running in the streets, chasing that money to bring it home to mommy."

"Yeah, you better hope that's all he's chasing and bringing home to mommy. Where you at?"

"Bitch, didn't I just tell your crazy ass I was at Capone's house 'bout to leave. Sha was over here, but she left. She said she wasn't going to be able to meet up with us tomorrow, but she still wanted to hook up with us during the weekend. I was about to jump in a cab and go over Summer's when I realized I left the keys at her house."

"I have a copy of her house keys. You can come get mines. I'ma leave them on the kitchen table and leave the front door open for you. I'm tired as shit."

"Penny, why are you sleeping so much lately?"

"I don't know. I hope I'm not pregnant."

"Bitch, please, you know you can't get pregnant from masturbation." They both started laughing.

"You see now, bitch, you trying to play me. What 'cha trying to say? That I don't get no dick? For your information, Bill Blast takes real good care of me."

"Girl, I hope you haven't been having unprotected sex with that nigga. And you know he fucks with them niggas from Smurf Village, the same niggas rumored to have killed Destiny."

118

"Yeah, but I know Blast didn't have nothing to do with that shit. He's not feeling them niggas, either. He feels like Spyda set Rashawn up. The only reason he's fucking with them is because he got his money out there. He told me once he flips his money, he's pulling out and he was going to get at that nigga Spyda for what happened to Rashawn."

"Have you told Summer that you fuck with Bill Blast?"

"Nah, I didn't want to tell her right now because I didn't know how she would take it, knowing he be with Spyda and them."

"Yeah, especially right now. At least wait until we find out who's really responsible. You know how she's carrying it. Everybody that was rumored to have some type of involvement she wants dead, and can you blame her?"

"Nah, I want them dead just as much as she does, but I know Bill Blast didn't have nothing to do with it. Besides, you know Bill Blast don't have the heart to kill no damn body."

"Anyway, girl, you're still crazy for having unprotected sex with these niggas today. Girl, you know they got some new shit out there now that don't respond to the medication, and that shit becomes full blown AIDS in two muthafuckin' months. They're calling that shit the super virus. And you know it's hitting our communities harder than anybody else's. You know how these young chickenhead girls is just giving it up to these nasty perverted niggas for a pair of sneakers and a blunt to smoke. They target niggas like Bill Blast who got money, a nice car, and are as slow as he is."

"Cookie, I know, girl, but the dick got good to me, and I think I got caught out there."

"Have you been to the doctor yet?"

"Nah, but I know my body, and I've been throwing up all day. Just my luck I'm pregnant by this nigga and we wind up having to kill this nigga. That's the type of luck I have with men."

"When was the last time you had your period?"

"I had it last month, but I haven't had it yet for this month, and it's past due. I'ma go to the doctor in the morning. My doctor is cool like that. She will let me just come in without making an appointment."

"Damn, girl, your ass is really pregnant."

"Cookie, I hope not."

"Have you told Aunty yet?"

"I'm not even sure if I am, and no, I haven't told nobody. You better keep your big mouth shut, too. For real, I don't want Summer to know until we find out who's responsible for what happened to Ms. Hardy and Destiny. Are you going to come and get my keys? If so, I'ma leave my front door open and they will be on the kitchen table."

"Yeah, I'm on my way."

"A'ight, Cookie, don't wake me when your ass gets here."

"You know I will. Bye!"

* * * * *

Big Ruben quickly turned around as he heard the patting of feet quickly approaching from behind. As he spun off of instincts, he pulled out his .40 caliber from his waist. He turned and was face-to-face with the two youngens he saw walking towards him when he got out of the truck. Big Ruben noticed both of them were holding heat. He looked up at Sha's Range as she turned the corner.

"Bitch!" Big Ruben said out loud, knowing he had been set up. Without hesitation, he fired.

POP...POP...POP...POP...

Immediately, loud gunshots echoed throughout the still night as both Big Ruben and Razor dropped. As Big Ruben hit the ground, Two-Guns Paul ran over, knelt over him, pointed his gun to Big Ruben's forehead, and pulled the trigger.

POP...POP...POP...

"That's for Black Supreme, nigga! Blood for life!" Two-Guns ran over to Razor. "Damn, Blood." Razor was already gone, dead before he hit the ground. Big Ruben had hit him directly between the eyes. Two-Guns took his red bandana out of his pocket and covered Razor's face with it before he took off running.

Chapter 9
Summer's Cold Heart

When Cookie walked in the house all the lights were off and the door was wide open. Cookie walked to Summer's room where she was laying across her bed fully dressed with her sneakers on in the bed and a gun lying on the pillow next to her head.

"*What the fuck is she doing with a gun lying next to her?*" Cookie thought to herself. Her next thought was that Summer was contemplating killing herself. *Does she have a death wish?* Cookie questioned as she entered Summer's room and walked towards her bed. Summer immediately jumped up, grabbing the gun and pointing it at Cookie.

"Summer, wait it's me!" Cookie screamed. "Don't shoot!"

With a blank stare, Summer held the gun with a steady but firm grip as she pointed it at Cookie's head. Realizing it was Cookie, she slowly lowered the gun. Cookie noticed Summer had tears in her eyes, as if she had been crying in her sleep.

"Summer, are you alright?" Cookie took the gun out of Summer's hands as she hugged her. "Summer, talk to me. What's wrong? You're scaring me."

"I'm sorry, Cookie, but I keep having visions and bad dreams of my sister and the night my parents were murdered. I can't get the horrible sight of Destiny and my grandmother's bodies out of my head. It's as if they're punishing me for not protecting Destiny."

"Come on, sis, you got to let go of the guilt. That's not healthy. You know Destiny don't blame you for her being murdered, and she knows you loved her more than life. So, please stop putting yourself through this abuse. Taking the burden of your family's murder is a heavy load that isn't healthy for you. You're going to drive yourself crazy."

"Cookie, it might already be too late for that. I have lost my whole family to these streets, and the images of their deaths haunt my thoughts. They can't rest in peace until I get who's responsible for this."

"Don't worry, Summer, time will tell all. Where did you get this big ass gun from that you almost shot my head off with?" Cookie looked at the gun with a spooked out stare.

"I took it from Lil' Justice."

Cookie looked at Summer with a puzzled look on her face, trying to figure out where she knew the name from. Then it hit her. "Little black-ass Justice?" Cookie asked.

"Yeah," Summer whispered. "I murdered him tonight and took his money and gun." Summer pointed to the stack of bills on the dresser.

"You did what? Girl, stop playing."

"Cookie, you know I'm not playing. I woke up from one of my bad dreams and went to a bar to try and clear my head. Just my luck, Justice approached me and tried to push up. He must not have recognized me. He even thought he was going to get some pussy. Therefore, I played his game, recognizing him the whole time. I knew he was one of

Spyda's main boys. So, I made him think I had just broken up with my man and was looking for some rebound sex. I knew I wanted to kill him, but I didn't know how I would kill him. I had no gun or nothing. He bought a bottle of Cristal before we left the bar and went to his house. When we got inside his house, I hit him over the head with the bottle, breaking it, and then I slit his throat from ear to ear with the broken bottle."

Looking at Summer in disbelief, Cookie couldn't believe what she had just told her. Summer sat on her bed with a cold stare as she looked into nothingness. "Girl, you're fucking serious!"

"Very, and I promise I won't stop until all the people who's rumored to have something to do with the murders is dead." Summer raised the gun once more to show Cookie she was serious. "And guess what? They will all die with one of their own guns."

"Summer, what about those that's innocent? You can't just kill everybody because of rumors."

"What about my grandmother and sister? They were innocent. My sistah was only sixteen. They didn't give a fuck about that. So, I don't give a fuck. I lost all of my heart the night I walked in this same house and saw the family I had slain and laying in their own blood. Fuck 'em! Guilt by association."

Cookie leaned over and gave Summer a hug. "Girl, you need a hug. Summer, I'm with you, but right now, I have to calm my nerves. I need to take my medicine." Cookie went into her purse and pulled out a folded up dollar bill. When she unfolded the bill, it was filled with cocaine.

"What's that?" Summer asked, knowing perfectly well what it was, but wanting to hear what Cookie would tell her.

"This is 'Girl' a.k.a. 'Blow' or 'Cocaine'. Do you wanna take a ride on this rollercoaster with me?"

"Nah, Cookie, my mind is already fucked up. That shit might take me some place I don't want to be." Summer gave Cookie a look of disbelief. "I still can't believe how much you and Penny have changed in the last three months. This shit must have always been in y'all, just waiting to let loose."

"I know, sis. We didn't know how or what to do without you. When you was put in the hospital, we was lost, and the only way to escape our fears was this shit…drugs and alcohol. I wish I never did any of this shit and stayed with school, but we was so worried about you we couldn't think straight. And you talking about you can't believe how much we have changed? Girl, you just blew my mind. You murdered a muthafucka! I can see shooting a person from a distance, but to damn near cut their head off with a broken bottle, it takes a person that's kinda loose upstairs to do that. Don't you think?" Cookie smiled at Summer as she sniffed the cocaine through a cut-off straw. Then, she passed it to Summer. "Come on, sis, we're in this for life."

"True that! Fuck it! Let me get that. I need something to help me sleep." Summer took the dollar bill and the straw, and she sniffed cocaine for the first time, actually enjoying it.

* * * * *

Butter Bean sat on his couch while 50 Cent's new album, *The Massacre*, played in the background. Passion laid her head between his lap, doing what she did best, pleasing Butter. She gripped his shaft with both hands as she slowly jerked his massive manhood and teased the head of his cock with short, wet kisses.

"Daddy, you know that I love pleasing you orally," Passion said as she went down on him and wrapped her lips around his entire hard-on, taking it all into her mouth, inch by inch.

"Mmmm, yes!" Butter grunted from the heat of Passion's mouth. "Yeah, right there, ma. I can tell you like doing this because you became a pro at pleasing daddy. That's what I like. Yeah, right there," Butter whispered.

Passion removed his manhood from her mouth, but continued to jerk him off with a tight grip. "Daddy, please fuck me tonight. I want you inside of me. I want you to be my first and only. My insides are burning for you," she begged as she took him into her mouth again. She licked from the base of his cock, up his shaft, and then took the head into her mouth while she gave his balls a little squeeze. Then, she took his cock out of her mouth once again. "Please, daddy, I'll do anything for you. I'll even kill them dudes from the old side for you so you won't have to worry about them no more."

Her words must have triggered something in Butter, because he lifted her up and ordered her to take off her clothes. She quickly undressed and then straddled his hard-on that was sticking straight up like six o'clock. As she straddled him, Butter knew she was nervous, because he could feel her trembling as she lowered herself on top of him. When the head of his manhood entered her, she let out a loud moan mixed with pleasure and pain.

126

"Oh, daddy, yes!" Passion wrapped her arms around Butter's neck and squeezed him tight as she rode his dick. She was so tight; he could feel she was having her first orgasm. Her body shook with convulsions as tears rolled down her face. Passion was stuck for words and was momentarily lost for breath. She couldn't believe the feeling she was experiencing. "Oh my God! Daddy, yes... fuck this virgin pussy!" she screamed as she bucked on top of him. Butter remained quiet while he maintained his control. The only way Passion could tell he was enjoying himself was from his heavy breathing. But right now, it didn't matter to her if he was enjoying himself because she was at the point of no return. "Daddy, I'm cumming again! Yes! Yes!" At that point, Butter felt he could release because he had given Passion the ultimate time that would have her locked for years. As Passion screamed from feeling Butter bust off inside of her, the front door came crashing down.

"What the fuck!" Butter pushed Passion off of him and tried to reach for his gun, which was lying on the coffee table. His first thought was that Spyda and his crew were moving in on him.

Before Butter could reach his heat, he felt a sharp pain in his side. As he fell to the floor, Justin jumped on top of him and started hitting him in the head with his cast. Passion screamed as she rushed Justin and started punching and scratching Justin's face trying to get him off of Butter. With no problem, Justin threw Passion off of him as he pulled out his 9mm and pointed it at her while he sat on top of Butter's chest, pinning his arms to the side.

"Don't move, bitch!" Justin screamed at Passion as he aimed at her head. Realizing she was only a kid, he told her to leave. "I'm the police! Get the fuck out of here!"

Passion snatched up her clothes off the floor, got dressed, and ran out the door. At that time, Butter was regaining consciousness.

"What the fuck!"

CRACK!

Justin hit his brother across the face with his gun.

"Ahhhhh!" Blood shot out of Butter's mouth and nose as he screamed and tried to cover his face from another hit. Butter's whole left side of his face went numb. Justin had his cast pressed up against his windpipe, stopping Butter's oxygen from reaching his brain and causing him to slowly slip back into unconsciousness.

"Muthafucka, if you ever send some of your lil' cronies at me again, I'ma send them back to you in a body bag. Then, I'm coming to see you. Consider this your last warning."

CRACK!

Justin smacked Butter across the face once more with his gun, knocking him totally unconscious. Justin then got up and walked out the house.

* * * * *

After Sha and Truman left his office, they went down to the jailhouse on Atlantic Avenue and bailed Spyda out. It took about a half hour before Spyda came out, and when he did, he looked like he had been through hell. His face was swollen and his right eye was shut from where the detectives had beaten him. Spyda shook Truman's hand and thanked him.

"Just remember, Spyda, your court date is next week. Make sure you show up, or there will be a warrant for your arrest and you'll lose your money." Truman shook both of their hands.

"A'ight, I got you, son. Thanks again." Spyda turned to Sha as Truman walked off. "Yo, what's up, ma? You see what them devils did to my face?"

"What they do? Try to kill you in there?"

"Nah, not in there…at the muthafuckin' precinct. The muthafuckin' devils at the 71st. I'm glad you came to get a nigga, though. I need you to hold me tonight."

"Spyda, I'm tired. I have to go home because I have something I have to do in the morning for my brother before I go see my parole officer." Sha reached into her bag and pulled out the extra two thousand left over from the money. "Here, this is what's left of the money I collected."

"What?! Come on, ma, you're not going to stay with a nigga?"

"Spyda, you know I would love to stay with you tonight, but I have a lot of running around to do in the morning. Plus, I'm tired. I've been running around all day trying to collect this money from your crew."

"Damn, Sha, you can't even consider giving a brotha a lil' bit of your time? I had a long night, too. The police beat the shit out of me; I had to punish a fool in the cell; plus, I have a new gun case that I might have to do some time for. Come on, Sha, the least you could do is let a nigga's night go out with a bang. And I mean a BANG!" Spyda gave Sha a pitiful smile, then grabbed her by the waist and sucked on her neck. "Come on, ma, you got a brother standing in front of the jail begging. Let's go rent a room across the street at the hotel and make passionate love."

"Okay, Spyda, but I can't stay all night." Sha had promised Bill Blast that she would come back and see him, but he could wait until another time. What she really wanted to know was the outcome with Big Ruben. She had told Butter that she would be back after she bailed Spyda out. As they walked across the street to the hotel, she turned to Spyda. "Oh yeah, Big Ruben said to call him as soon as you got released."

"Yeah, he'll have to wait until later because technically I haven't been released yet. I'm still a prisoner of lust," Spyda replied while grabbing Sha's ass as they walked into the hotel lobby.

*   *   *   *   *

As Justin drove from Butter's apartment, his mind drifted. The situation with his brother and the murders was becoming overwhelming. There had always been bad blood between him and his brothers, which mainly stemmed from him having a different father. Therefore, they blamed him for the abuse his father put them through. From this day on, however, Justin no longer considered Butter his brother, and he knew Butter would treat him as his sworn enemy, as well.

When Justin first joined the force, this enhanced Butter's hatred of him. Butter was the only one who knew what Justin had done, but he never told because he knew his older brother would have put Justin on the hit list. Because Butter and Justin were closest in age, Butter had a little more love for his younger brother. When Justin found out that his older brothers were responsible for the murders of the couple at the club eight years ago, he had snitched on his brothers and told the police where the guns were stashed. Butter knew it was Justin that told, because besides the older brothers and Butter, Justin had watched them as they stashed the guns in the basement. When the police came to the house, they went right to the basement and got the dirty guns out of a spot no one would have ever looked unless they knew where to look. So, that created a distance between the two.

Justin knew his family was responsible for the two young girl's parents being dead. Therefore, he felt it was his responsibility to bring the killer to justice even if it was his own brother and his crew of fake thugs. Justin felt somewhat obligated to Summer because once again, his family had been implemented in the deaths of the same family, not to mention the feelings he was starting to have for Summer.

Justin's thoughts were broken by the dispatcher over the police radio. "We have a 187, two confirmed dead. A possible gang dispute on Macon and Malcolm X Boulevard."

"Damn! This shit won't ever end," Justin thought to himself as he activated the police lights on top of the unmarked vehicle, made a U-turn, and headed back in the direction from which he had just came.

* * * * *

As soon as Passion got outside, she ran to a payphone and called Dice. While she waited for Justin to leave, she watched from the corner. When Justin was out of sight, she ran back in the house to find Butter lying unconscious on the floor, bleeding from his mouth and nose. She panicked and started screaming, thinking he was dead. She ran over and cradled his head against her breast as he started regaining consciousness.

"Oh, daddy, you're alive!" Passion screamed while tears of joy fell from her eyes.

Butter tried to get up, but fell back to the floor. His knees were weak and his coordination was fucked up. The blows to his head had him not knowing whether he was coming or going. Passion grabbed him in her arms.

"Daddy, don't move. Lay here for a minute."

"Passion, what the fuck happened?" Butter asked, confused.

"A cop kicked in the door and started hitting you with his gun and cast. He had a broken arm. I tried to get 'em off of you, but he was too strong for me. He pushed me to the floor, pointed his gun at me, and told me to get the fuck out. I heard him say something about the next time you send your soldiers after him he'll send them back in a body bag. Daddy, do you know that cop?" As soon as Passion told him that, Butter knew it had been his brother.

Butter got up enough strength to sit up, and Passion helped him to the couch, "Daddy do you want some water?" she asked as she went into the bathroom and got him a rag to fill with ice for his face. Passion returned to the living room. "Here, daddy, put this on your face. I called Dice, and he's on his way."

* * * * *

A block away from Butter's house, Dice's cell phone rang.

"Yo, who's this?"

"Dice, the nigga Ruben is dead, but he killed Razor and the two lil' homies got knocked. That nigga Diekman clapped both of them. I'm at the Pj's, now and the nigga's sistah just told me that he was hit in the stomach and is being charged with the assault on a police officer."

"Meet me at Butter's crib now. Some shit just jumped off with that nigga Diekman."

"A'ight."

CLICK...

Chapter 10
After Summer Comes Fall

Sha slowly and seductively undressed while turning her back to face Spyda. She walked to the bed as her naked 5'3", 125 pound, curvaceous frame glared from the light of the TV. Spyda admired every curve of Sha's perfect 10 body.

"Damn, girl! You sure you can't stay with a nigga tonight?" Spyda asked as he advanced to the bed while Sha lay with her legs spread apart.

"No, but I am sure we can enjoy the time we can spend together." Sha smiled while opening her legs further apart as if inviting him to come and eat up.

Spyda undressed and crawled between her legs as he lay on his stomach Sha tried not to look at Spyda's face, afraid the swelling of his lip would turn her off. Spyda placed both of his arms under her legs, resting them on his shoulders, and slowly started parting her womanhood with his tongue; he gently licked as he allowed his tongue to explore.

"Oh, yes!" Sha moaned as she tossed her head back and closed her eyes, enjoying Spyda's touch. As Spyda hit the right spots with his tongue, Sha gasped for air as her mouth fell open, but she couldn't utter any words. One of Spyda's best qualities was him knowing how to give ultimate pleasure to the cat. Not only was he a master cocksmith, but his tongue was also platinum.

Sha clasped her hands on Spyda's head so she could control his movement, and forced his face deeper into her pussy. Spyda didn't back down from Sha's challenge, though. He gave quick little jabs at her clit with the tip of his tongue and sucked on it by pulling it into his mouth momentarily and then releasing it, sending electrifying shockwaves throughout her entire body. As he flicked his tongue and played with the clitoris, he fingered her with three fingers.

"Oh my God! Yes, nigga! Eat this pussy good!" Sha grunted and moaned as she shivered uncontrollably "Oh yes, muthafucka! I'm cumming!"

"Yeah, baby girl! That's what I want you to do. Let me taste your love juices." Spyda said as he moved his tongue freely from the inner folds of her vaginal lips to the outer, while keeping his entire mouth over her womanhood. As Sha's hot sticky cum covered Spyda's mouth, he slightly hummed to send low vibration sensations to her vagina.

"Did you enjoy that, ma?" he asked as he slowly turned Sha on to her stomach.

"Mmm, you know I did." Sha quickly raised her ass up in the air. She knew exactly what Spyda's freaky ass wanted to do next.

"Ma, I'm not finished with you yet. I know what you like, and I'm going to please you."

"You think I don't know what you like doing? Don't talk about it; be about it." Sha giggled as she raised her ass up and fingered herself. Spyda slowly massaged her perfectly heart-shaped firm ass as he kissed and licked each cheek. He even licked in between them and around her asshole. He tapped at the opening of her anal canal with the tip of his tongue, preparing her, and then going full throttle, he started to thrust his tongue in and out of her ass.

"Oh yes, you nasty muthafucka! Toss my salad. Clean my ass." Sha talked dirty to Spyda as he ate the ass nonstop and she continued to play with herself, bringing herself to another climax. Sha's cell phone started vibrating on the table. "Hold up, daddy, let me get my phone before it falls of the table from vibrating." Sha attempted to get up.

"Ma, fuck that damn phone. I'll buy you another one." Spyda grabbed Sha and prevented her from getting up.

"I got to answer that. It might be important, or they wouldn't be calling my phone this late."

"What? Man, let that shit ring. If it's really important, they'll call back."

"Hold up one minute, Spyda." Sha got up, walked over to the table, and answered her phone. Spyda laid on the bed watching and admiring Sha's build as he slowly stroked his manhood, patiently waiting for her to return to the bed.

"Hello."

"Yo, Sha, this is Kevin. Is Spyda with you?"

"Yeah."

"Can you put him on the phone?"

"Hold on." Sha walked over to the bed and passed Spyda the phone.

"Who's this?" he asked while accepting the phone from her.

"It's Kevin."

"Son, they killed Big Ruben!"

"What?! When?"

"Son, that's not all. They found lil' Justice dead in his apartment. Somebody damn near cut his head off."

"What?! Get the fuck out of here!"

"Yo, the po-po is out here going crazy. And get this; Ruben murdered one of the cats before he was murked. The nigga was Blood."

"Yo, Kevin, I'm on my way to the crib. Have everybody meet me at the crib on Underhill."

"A'ight, see ya when I get there. One!"

Spyda pressed the talk button on the cell phone and then passed the phone back to Sha.

"Spyda, is everything okay?"

"Nah, niggas just murdered Big Ruben and Justice. Get dress; we got to go."

* * * * *

RING...RING...RING...
RING...RING...RING...

Penny sat up in her bed and tried to focus on the digital clock radio that sat on her dresser. *Who in the fuck is calling my house at three-fifteen in the morning?"* Penny thought as she climbed out of bed and walked over to her phone, snatching it up. "What!" she answered with an attitude.

"Damn, ma, it's like that. A nigga's trying to set up a booty call. What's up?"

"Bill Blast?!"

"Who else would you have calling this time of morning talking about setting up a booty call? Girl, you bet not play with me."

"Nah, I was just asleep. I'm not feeling well."

"Then you're in luck, because Doctor Feelgood called right on time. Let a nigga come over and do them things you like to make you feel better."

"Blast, I have a doctor's appointment in the morning."

"What's wrong with you?"

"I think I'm pregnant!"

"What? By who?"

"Bill Blast, don't even play me like that. Who the fuck you think? By your ass, nigga."

"Whoa, ma, I apologize. I'm on my way right now."

* * * * *

"Yo, Murder, we got to meet everybody up at Butter's crib. Some shit jumped off."

"Two-Guns, what's poppin?" Murder asked as him and Bloody Dog walked up to the mini-van that Two-Guns Paul was driving.

"Shit jumped off. Come on y'all get in so we can go get the rest of the people. I just spoke to Dice." Bloody Dog and Murder jumped in the van.

"Yo, you know Half Pint and Gutter got knocked off at the game room today." Lil' Murder said as he pulled out a Dutch master and started unwrapping the leaf.

"Yeah, I know. Yo, you know we hit that nigga Big Ruben tonight?"

"Word! Yeah, that nigga had cats under pressure, ya heard. Who hit him?"

"Me and Razor."

Two-Guns Paul pointed under the seat and told Murder to pass him the bottle of Bacardi underneath. After

Murder passed the bottle, Two-Guns tilted the bottle up to his head as he drove.

"Word, dog! Y'all got that nigga, huh?"

"Yeah, but Razor was hit. He's dead."

"Aw, man! What the fuck!"

"Yeah, and Trife and that lil' nigga Running Joe got popped today, too. They was sent to rough that nigga Diekman up, but he clapped both of them. Now they're facing charges of assault and attempted murder of a police officer."

"Man, what the fuck! Shit is crazy," Murder said as he passed the perfectly rolled Dutch to Bloody Dog to light.

"Some shit jumped off, but I don't know what. Dice just told me to go to the Pj's to get the crew and let them know to meet at Butter's crib. So I'ma take a few, and y'all tell the rest what's going down."

Ten minutes later, Two-Guns pulled up in front of the building where a couple of the fellas were standing.

"What's up, Damu?" one of the young'ns said as they all acknowledged the van. Two-Gun, Murder, and Bloody Dog all got out and walked up to where they were standing.

"Yo, Butter wants all the lieutenants to meet at his crib. Yo, Beast, you and your crew hold it down until we get back. I'ma take the upstate crew with me. Some shit went down, so be on point out here."

"Yo, them po-po from the 71st came through talking about if the Bloods want war, we got it. Then, they pulled off. After they left, the Damus from the 77th came through and told us to be careful because Diekman and the boys at 71st got it out for us. They said the 71st is gunning for the whole clique, and they said it was because of some of our boys trying to kill Diekman."

139

"Yo, don't sweat that; we got that. Y'all just be on point and we'll fill y'all in on everything when we get back."

"A'ight, Blood. One!"

Two-Gun, Murder, and five other soldiers all jumped in the van, while Blood Dog stayed behind with Beast and the rest of the crew.

* * * * *

Bill Blast pulled up to the light. With his mind on what Penny had just told him, he paid no attention to the unmarked car pulling up behind him. Bill Blast's thoughts were interrupted by the flashing of lights and a siren. He looked through his rearview mirror and the detectives motioned for him to pull over.

Whoop! Whoop!

"Damn, these muthafuckas!" Bill Blast immediately recognized the D's from the 77th precinct and knew they were on the Bloods payroll. As Bill Blast pulled over to the curb, the D's jumped out with their guns pointed and screaming as they ran up to the car.

"Don't move, bitch! Let me see your muthafuckin' hands before I shoot you in your ugly ass face."

"Officer, what did I do?"

"Shut up and get the fuck out the car. If your ass flinches, I'ma shoot your ass good where your mother won't recognize you. Now get the fuck out!" The detective snatched Bill Blast out of the car while his partner held his gun pointed at Bill Blast's head the whole time. The short detective threw him up against the car and frisked him down.

"Officer, I didn't do nothing," Bill Blast pleaded, hoping they wouldn't check the car.

"What's going on with all the shooting around here lately? I know you know something. You have beef with some Bloods?"

"Man, I don't know nothing, officer, and I don't have no beef with nobody. I was just on my way to my girl's house."

"Yeah right, you look like the type that was riding around scheming. You're down with Spyda and his crew, ain't 'cha?" the detective asked as he reached in Bill Blast's pocket and pulled out a wad of money.

"Nah, officer, I don't know no Spyda, and I wasn't scheming on nobody." Bill Blast started getting nervous as the other detective searched the car. He prayed the detective wouldn't find the drugs, but Bill Blast knew he would because the bag was in plain view.

"What the hell you doing with this type of money on you at this time of morning?"

"I told you, officer, I was going to my girl's house."

"Are you sure you're not one of Spyda's boys? I could be mistaken, but I know I saw you with them on the new side a couple of times."

"Bingo!" the detective searching the car said as he stood up with a Tec 9. "Look what he had in his car under the seat."

"I guess you needed that for protection from your girlfriend?" the detective said sarcastically as he started putting handcuffs on Bill Blast. Bill Blast just put his head down as the other detective stood back up again, but this time he had a bag.

"We have something else." The detective went into the bag and pulled out an eighth of cocaine and about a quarter pound of weed. "Well, well, well, we have us a big player in the game," the detective said as he laid the drugs on the hood of the car. "Goddamn! Boy, you a real baller. How much money and drugs is here? Your ass is going down. Now listen here, mister, you can make it easier for yourself and tell us what's going down tonight and we'll give you back your money, drugs, and your gun, plus let you go. We just wanna know if y'all plan on making a move on the new side tonight."

Bill Blast didn't say a word; he just kept his head down.

"Alright, you know what? Call a patrol car to transport his ass to jail," the short detective told his partner.

"Consider yourself lucky tonight. These drugs are too much paperwork, so we'll make this disappear for you, and we'll keep the money as our payment for doing this for you. But the gun, your ass is going down for it. And when you get out, come see me and I'll resell it to you for a cheap price." The detective smiled at Bill Blast as he made him sit on the ground until the patrol car came for transport.

The detective who found the drugs and gun opened the wrapped cocaine and took a sniff. "Ahhh! That's some good shit right there." He passed the package to his partner, who took one fingernail full and sniffed.

"Yo, you're right. This shit is the bomb. We better put this up before the boys in blue come. We're going to have some fun with some stripper bitches tonight. Thanks to you, of course." The detective put the drug package in their car as the patrol car with two uniformed cops was pulling up.

*   *   *   *   *

Passion opened the door for Dice,
What's up, Passion? Where's Butter?"

"He's in the back."

"A'ight," When Dice walked to the back room
Butter Bean was laid on his bed with the ice rag on his
head. With Butter's whole face swollen, he looked like
Martin on that episode when he fought Tommy "the hit
man" Hermes. Butter's shit was twisted. "Yo, Damu, you
a'ight?" Dice asked as he walked up to the bed.

Butter took the ice off of his head and sat up. "Yo,
that nigga got to pay for this shit. I should have killed this
nigga long ago."

Passion walked into the room with a blunt already
rolled and lit. She passed the blunt to Butter. Dice could
smell the dust.

"Dog, for real, I have to kill this nigga. He violated
me," Butter said as he inhaled the smoke.

"Son, we just can't kill no police officer like that.
Plus, the nigga is your brother." Passion's mouth dropped
open when she heard that. She couldn't believe the police
that had damn near beat the death out of Butter was
actually his brother.

"Daddy, I'll kill him."

"What?" Butter and Dice both turned around and
looked at Passion. Passion wanted to make up for leaving
Butter earlier. She wanted to show him that she would kill
for him.

"Daddy, I can murder him and make it seem like he
tried to rape me. I'll say we met over the internet and he
invited me over. And when I refused to have sex with him,
he started hitting me and pulled out his gun. During the
struggle, I murdered him. Who do you think they're going

to believe, a sixteen-year-old or a corrupt cop?" Passion said as she sat down next to Butter.

"Yeah, but Diekman ain't corrupt," Dice replied.

"No, but she can plant some drugs in the house," Butter said as he passed Dice the blunt.

"Nah, Blood, you know I don't fuck with that shit. Strictly weed. Yo, you serious about this?"

"Yeah, nigga, look at my face! Plus, that nigga snitched on our brothers about them bodies years ago. I'm the only one who knew he did that shit but didn't say nothing because I knew they would have sic the dogs on him. He was the only thing I had left, so I kept that shit to myself…but the nigga is no longer my brother in my eyes. He's a snake rat ass that needs to get his cap pushed back."

"Yeah, but if we do this shit, nobody can know but us three. We can't even tell the homies, because when it comes to a police being killed after there was an earlier attempt on his life, it will bring a lot of pressure. And you know pressure busts pipes."

As they spoke about their next move and how they were going to go about it, the doorbell rang. So, they stopped talking about what they were planning until everybody left.

Chapter 11
Only Two Seasons: Summer and Winter

Sha dropped Spyda off at the crib on Underhill.

"Yo, Sha, get at me tomorrow so we can finish where we left off." Spyda went into his pocket and handed Sha a G note from the two G's left of the bail money. Then, he leaned over, gave her a kiss on the cheek, got out of the truck, and walked into the building.

As Sha pulled off, she pulled out her cell phone to call Butter. She wanted to know what the verdict was.

"Yo! Who's this?"

"Butter, it's me, Sha."

"What's up, baby girl?"

"I'm hoping you tell me. Is everything alright? I heard one of your people was murdered."

"Yeah, but sometimes sacrifice is needed to get our man. That's what counts. But some other shit popped off. Are you coming by?"

"Nah, not tonight. I have a lot of running around to do for my brother in the morning. I'll call you later when I finish what I'm doing."

"A'ight, ma, get at me tomorrow. One!"

CLICK...

* * * * *

Butter walked back into the living room and put the ice pack back on his head to reduce the swelling. After pouring himself straight vodka, he sat next to Dice.

"Dice, was it our people who hit Justice?"

"Not that I know of." Dice looked at Two-Guns Paul and lil' Murder to see if they knew anything about it. They both shook their heads no.

"Who do you think did that shit?"

"Man, you know that nigga Justice was a real shiesty dude. He had a whole nation gunning for his ass. One of them five percenter cats could have got at him. Everybody wanted that nigga dead," Two-Guns said as he passed lil' Murder the blunt.

"Fuck 'em! That's just one less muthafucka we have to get. Two down, now who else?" Dice asked.

"What about them niggas Bill Blast and Kevin?" Butter inquired.

"Kevin is pussy; he's no threat gun-wise, but he's a hustler. When it comes to gun play, you won't ever see him. He's like the brain behind Spyda. If we snatch that nigga up, he'll tell us whatever we want to know. Trust me, I went to school with that nigga, and he's straight pussy like that." Known for reading people through their reactions and body movement, Dice watched everybody's facial expression for a reaction to what he had just said. He was on some real art of war shit; he wanted the crew to fight this war like a game of chess. He also knew Sha was the Queen and that Spyda was actually a pawn. "Besides, everybody knows that the only time Kevin has any heart is when he gets drunk. Then he wants to play with guns. But that can work on our behalf, because when the nigga gets drunk, he gets reckless."

Butter was feeling what Dice was saying, which was one of the reasons Dice was one of his top men, because the boy planned his every action carefully.

"Yo, Blood, I'll snatch that nigga up," Two-Guns Paul said as he got up, walked to the table, and poured himself a drink.

Two-Guns Paul was given the name back in 1989 when three dudes tried to stick him up for his three-quarter length Shearling coat and gold chain. Two-Guns was only fourteen at the time. The three dudes got the drop on Two-Guns and pulled out heat on him. Two-Guns was on the corner counting some money after just making a sale to a basehead, when the dudes ran up on him. They patted him down and took his gun he had in his coat pocket. They stripped him of his money, drugs, gold chain, and coat. However, as they turned to leave, Two-Guns pulled out a 9mm from his waist and started dumping on them, dropping all three of them. As he collected his shit, he told them that he always kept two guns on him. From that day forward everybody called him Two-Guns Paul.

"A'ight, Blood, take a couple of the homies and handle that. We got to end this shit quick because it's been going on too long. And what about Bill Blast?" Butter asked.

"That nigga Bill Blast is sneaky, but at the same time, he's not feeling that nigga Spyda. I know that chick Penny he fucks with. She's friends with my lil' sister and comes over the house sometimes. I heard her tell my sister that Bill Blast doesn't trust Spyda; he thinks Spyda had something to do with Rashawn, that ill-bitch Destiny, and her grandmother's murders. So we don't have to worry about him…I don't think. But to be on the safe side, we can get that nigga, too." Dice once again waited for a response before he finished what he was saying. "We can't sleep on that nigga Capone either. It's something about that nigga. He makes me feel funny. I use to always see the nigga, and now you never see that nigga nowhere."

"Nah, that nigga ain't no threat. I'm fucking his sister."

"Yeah, Butter, and you know that bitch…pardon me…but she's shiesty. Sha's more gangsta than all them niggas. I won't put it pass her that she's the one behind all of this just so her and her brother can take control of the drug flow around here. That's just my opinion."

"I feel you, Dice, but I don't think so. She was the one that set the shit up with Big Ruben."

"Butter, what's up with this shit with your brother Diekman? He fucked your shit up, Blood," Murder asked as he looked at Butter's face.

"Nothing, I'ma let that shit go. We have bigger fish to fry. My brother is a sucker." Butter didn't want any of the crew to know what him, Passion, and Dice planned on doing. The less muthafuckas that knew, the better. "Yo, did y'all hear anything from Half Pint or Gutter?" Butter asked quickly, changing the subject.

"Nah, not yet. They haven't gotten in touch with nobody yet, but I do know they had all that shit you just sent by Passion in the spot when the police raided it."

"What about Trife and the other homies?" Butter inquired.

"They'll live, but they're facing some time for the assault on a police officer," Dice informed him.

"Damn! So our next move is Kevin?"

"Yeah."

"A'ight, let's keep the pressure on these niggas' necks." Butter left out the living room and went in the bedroom with Passion, who was asleep. He woke her, wanting to finish what he had started before he was interrupted by Justin.

* * * * *

When Spyda walked into the crib, Kevin, the dyke broad Judy, Tec, and three other soldiers were all sitting on the couch smoking weed and playing video games. Spyda looked around the room, and that's when it hit him that Big Ruben was really dead. Big Ruben was the backbone of all of them. "Yo, where is that nigga Bill Blast?"

"I've been trying to reach the nigga since earlier. He hasn't returned my calls yet," Kevin said as he got up and gave Spyda a pound.

"Word? You sure nothing happened to him?"

"The last time I seen him was when I sent him with Sha to get the money to bail you out. Spyda, on the real though, I don't really trust that nigga Bill Blast. You know he's not from the Pj's, so he really don't care. I know he's jealous of you. He feels like he should have gotten the position you hold. And that nigga Capone, I haven't seen him either. I know you don't want to hear what I'm about to tell you, but that nigga's sistah Sha was seen creeping with that nigga Butter. Judy saw her a couple of days ago with the nigga, and that bitch know the drama we're going through with that nigga and his people."

"Word, Judy? You see her with that nigga and you didn't tell me?"

"I haven't seen you. I had to go make that move to collect and drop off in Ohio. I just got back today and heard all this shit. That's when I remembered and told Kevin."

"Spyda, that bitch probably set Big Ruben up. She was the last one to see him," Kevin said.

Spyda didn't want to believe what he was hearing, but he knew he couldn't put it pass her. She was shiesty and straight street, plus he knew she somewhat believed he had something to do with Rashawn's murder. She had to be murdered just for the suspicion of the crew. If he didn't, they would view that as a sign of weakness and he would lose favor in their eyes. He couldn't have that because he needed all of their trust if he wanted to win this war.

Looking at his crew, he said, "Then her ass is out. I'll take care of her myself."

"Yo, Spyda, the streets is on fire right now. The police is down our throat, especially the 77th with them niggas putting them on us. It's hard to eat right now. I have a couple of spots I want to look into in Brownsville that some of my boys from out there was telling me about, but they don't have the drugs to put in the spots. Their main supplier got knocked and they was left for dead. They said they got the manpower but no work. What do you want me to do?" Tec said as he passed the blunt to him.

"Yeah, that sounds good. We shut down most of the activities for awhile around the projects and open up new spots until this shit is over or dies down. Kevin, go with Tec to meet these dudes tomorrow."

"A'ight."

After calling a cab, Spyda left out the door to go home to Queens. What they just told him about Sha kind of fucked him up because he was feeling her, but now he had to get at her.

150

* * * * *

Half Pint sat handcuffed in the interrogation room in a hard ass chair for hours, staring at the dingy, off-white walls. The room had a gloomy feel to it. This was the room where many men were broken. Half Pint sat in the chair falling asleep when Detective Diekman and Detective Kenneth walked into the room. Diekman sat across from Half Pint, and Kenneth stood up behind him, leaning on the wall.

"Man, y'all had a lot of crack in the spot. Not to mention all of them damn assault riffles. What was y'all preparing for? The revolution?" Justin smiled at Half Pint. "Man, y'all stored and sold all them damn guns in a game room where little kids hung out. Half, you're a convicted felon with a firearm. Do you know what that means? The feds! The big boys!"

Half Pint remained silent, never once looking up at Justin, who threw a stack of pictures on the table of Destiny, Ms. Hardy, Rashawn, Hunt, Chuck, and Black Supreme. The last three pictures are what caught Half Pint's attention the most. He dropped his head. They were of Big Ruben, Justice, and Razor. He felt bad about the lil' homie Razor, but seeing Big Ruben and Justice caused him to smile.

"Do these images of death bring a smile to your face, Half Pint?"

Half Pint looked up at Justin for the first time. "Man, I still can't believe you. You must have forgotten who protected you all these years. The Bloods is the reason you're not dead. And now you're flipping and biting the same hands that tucked you in at night."

"Man, Half Pint, I'm not the one who's killing our own people with these senseless killings over colors and turf, that's all. You have been banging since I've known you. When is this shit going to stop?" Justin pointed at the pictures and pushed Destiny and Razor's pictures towards him. "Look at that. They both were only sixteen. And Razor, you Blooded him in, didn't you?"

"Yeah, but this is all me and the homies now, and we prefer death before dishonor."

"Do you really think this young kid wanted death? Look at 'em." Justin tapped on the picture. "Does this look like the face of somebody that wanted this? Y'all must stop fooling y'all selves and brainwashing our children."

"Man, Justin...oh my bad, Detective Diekman! Y'all are the ones brainwashed, and your conflict ain't with me. It's with your own self, and you know why, too. Everybody knows what you did to your own family. You are a sellout."

"Okay, Half Pint, I see this is about to go somewhere else. Let's put it like this. What can you do? Not for me, but yourself. What do you know about any of these murders? As of now, you're facing a lot of years, and you have eight children, don't you? Who's going to take care of them children for you? My brother don't give a fuck about you. He'll just get some other lil' lowlife that is willing to do his bidding for him because they believe that it's the code of the streets. Be for real. Look at what happened to the two lil' homies he sent after me. Do you think he cared about them?" Half Pint looked at Justin with a confused look on his face. "Oh, you didn't know, huh? Why you think I have this cast on my arm? Because my brother sent two of y'all lil' homies to teach me a lesson. But, of course, you know how it went down. The both of

152

them is laid up in the hospital with gunshot wounds to the stomach and charged with assault on a police officer. So I hope you're smarter than they are. Only you can help yourself."

Half Pint broke out in a loud laugh. "Yo, Justin, you are the funniest. You of all people know I'm not cut from that cloth. You must have lost your rabbit-ass mind. Why would you talk to me like this? Have I ever disrespected you? So why would you come to me with such disrespect? Man, take me back to the holding cell until it's time for me to go see the judge." Half Pint stood up as he looked Justin in his eyes. "Listen, Detective Justin Diekman, you do you, and the Bloods are going to do us!"

At that time, Detective Barton entered the room, walked over, and whispered something in Justin's ear. Barton left the room as quickly as he came, and Justin smiled as he stood up.

"Your boy Gutter is willing to make a deal. The funny thing is that he's not smart enough to know the police can't make a deal with him...only the D.A. You better make your decision quick because soon we might not need you."

Justin walked out the room followed by Kenneth.

* * * * *

RING...RING...RING...

"Capone, get the phone," Isis said as she gave him a slight nudge.

Isis was one of Capone's baby's mothers. He had a five-year-old son by her, but they weren't together. Yesterday was their son Donavan's birthday party, and he decided to let them stay the night after Sha and everybody had left. Isis had a way of getting what she wanted out of Capone, and she wanted him to buy her a new car for her and their son, so she seduced him. Isis was one of the baddest chicks around besides Sha and Summer, but she had a stink attitude, not to mention she belonged to the itty bitty titty committee, which was her only two flaws. They had been separated for over a year now, but continued to sleep with each other, which made shit even more complicated because of the feelings they still shared for each other. Isis was extremely jealous because she knew Capone was in a relationship with Cookie, so Isis used their son to get at Capone. Isis played like she was cool with Cookie, but on the real, she hated her. When Cookie showed up at their son's birthday party, she was furious, but when Cookie left, it was all good again and she was up in Capone's face smiling.

RING...RING...RING...

"Capone, get up and get your phone!" Isis started shaking Capone, trying to wake him, but he didn't budge. She knew Capone didn't want her to answer his phone because he didn't want Cookie to know she had stayed the night. And because of that, Isis stopped trying to wake Capone and answered the phone, hoping it was Cookie.

"Hello."

"Let me speak with Capone."

"Hold on." Isis smiled as she walked back over to the bed. "Capone...Capone, get up. It's your bitch!"

Hearing that, Capone jumped up and gave Isis a look that said if looks could kill she would be dead. He snatched the phone from her. "Hello!"

"Who that fucking hoe calling a bitch? And you still fucking her?" Cookie asked.

154

"Nah, I just came in. Her and my son stayed the night because she got drunk at the party and couldn't drive home."

Isis rolled her eyes, left the room, and went into the next room with Donavan.

"Yeah, whatever, nigga. I'm calling just to let you know shit is getting carried away. I'm at Summer's house and she just killed that nigga Justice. She's going after everybody rumored to have anything to do with that shit."

"Don't worry about nothing. Everything is going to be okay."

"They just had on the news that it's a full-blown war between the Bloods, the police, and other local street thugs. They said there have been over ten deaths and apparent shootings connected to the war, and even an assault on the police."

"Listen, Cookie, we don't have nothing to worry about. Let them kill each other, and then we'll step in and clean up. I didn't mean for it to go down the way it did, but it did. I don't need you losing your head on me now. Just be easy and everything is gonna come out the way we planned it. Just be easy."

"Capone, I just don't ever want Summer to find out anything or that I had anything to do with it."

"Listen, baby, just be easy."

"Capone, won't you come and get me?"

"Come on, Cookie, you know Isis and my son is over here."

"And! It's not like she can't be there by herself. What? You fucking her or something?"

"Nah, I already told you what happened. Don't start that shit again."

"So come over. I'm feeling horny. I want some dick."

"Damn! Since you put it like that, I'll be right over."

"A'ight, don't make me wait forever."

"Peace!"

CLICK...

As soon as Capone ended the call, Isis walked back into the room butt naked. When she climbed on top of Capone and started sucking on his neck, he pushed her off of him; he definitely had no desire to have a hicky. Capone then stood up and went into the bathroom.

"Capone, where are you going? That bitch calls and you just gonna leave me and your son like this? You some real shit. You know what? Fuck you, nigga!" Isis screamed as she picked up his cell phone and threw it at the door.

"Bitch! You better calm the fuck down!" Capone came charging out the bathroom as Isis turned his 50-inch flat screen TV over onto the floor. Capone grabbed Isis and they started tussling as they both fell to the floor.

"Get off of me!" Isis screamed as she started swinging wildly.

Capone knew only one thing would calm her down, so he started kissing and sucking on her neck and chest. Isis immediately responded while returning the kisses. Her screams quickly became soft moans as Capone went down on her right in the middle of the floor.

Chapter 12
Summer's Heat

Summer awoke from another one of her dreams, which were occurring more frequently. This one, however, was detailed to the point where she could almost see what Destiny saw the night of the murders. One of the images in her dream was that of a woman, whose face was blurred. Summer sat up in her bed, once again sweating profusely.

"Damn! What was this dream about?" Summer questioned herself as she got out of the bed and walked into the bathroom to wet her face "Why was there an image of a female standing over Destiny's body? That is the first time I ever had that dream." While brushing her teeth, Summer pondered her latest dream. "Is Destiny trying to tell me something?"

Afterwards, Summer went into the kitchen to fix herself a cup of coffee, hoping it would help with her hangover. While sitting at the table drinking her cup of black coffee, she turned on the TV and watched the news. Summer looked at the clock on the wall, and for the first time, she realized she had slept the majority of the day away. It was already after six o'clock in the evening. The news was flooded with the same things: sex, money, politics, murder and Michael Jackson's case. However, one story caught her attention.

A female news reporter stood live in front of the projects where she said an ongoing war with two sides of the same project had already claimed a dozen lives, including an assault on Detective Justin Diekman, who is the brother of Butter Bean, the leader of the Blood gang.

Summer froze; she couldn't believe what she had just heard. She put her coffee down and paid close attention to the broadcast. What she said next really bugged Summer out. The reporter continued by saying Detective Justin Diekman's older brothers were also responsible for the deaths of inspiring up and coming R&B singer Lyric and her husband B-Real at a nightclub eight years ago. The news anchor reported that the Feds were now involved with the case because there's possible police corruption involved in all levels of the case. She stated Officer Diekman was not believed to be involved with the corruption, but his brother is believed to be in the middle of a police scandal involving detectives of the 77th precinct, and the sources say the police have two suspects in other murders that are willing to cooperate.

Summer turned the TV off; she couldn't believe what she just had heard. She had slept with the brother of the men who had killed her mother and father and possibly the brother of the person responsible for taking the lives of her sister and grandmother.

Summer jumped up from the table and ran to the back to wake Cookie. Summer figured Cookie was still in Destiny's room asleep, but the room was empty and the bed was made.

"Cookie must have left last night or this morning," Summer said to herself as she went into her room to page her. As she reached the dresser, the phone started ringing.

Summer jumped, the phone scaring her, and she answered on the second ring.

"Hello!"

"Summer, I need to speak to you."

Summer's heart nearly stopped when she recognized the voice; it was Justin.

"About what? The fact that your family killed my parents and you never mentioned that to me? Justin, I trusted you."

"Listen, Summer, I didn't want you to find out like this. Please, I know how you must feel right now. Let me come over and talk to you, please. I can tell you everything. I'm not like my brothers. I am the one who turned them in eight years ago, and I promise you if my brother is re-sponsible for your sister's life, he will pay. Please, Summer, just give me a chance to explain where I stand. I would never hurt you or your family. That's why I made sure I visited you as much as I could when you were in the hospital. I felt somewhat obligated to protect you. After that night I met you at the precinct, I grew close to you and became even closer to you each time I visited you at the hospital, even though you didn't respond to my presence."

"So, Justin, why didn't you tell me and allow me to make the decision for myself whether I wanted to sleep with the person related to the people who destroyed my life? If I didn't hear it on the news, would you have told me?"

"Summer, I didn't know how to tell you. I wanted to, but I couldn't because I didn't want you to look at me in the same light as my family. Summer, please understand that I'm different; I'm not them monsters."

"Justin, you deceived me and my family, and I never want to see you again or I will take my revenge for my mother and father's lives out on *you*. Because you gave your brothers up to the authorities, it's you who made it impossible for me to give them the justice they deserved. DEATH!" No longer wanting to hear what Justin had to say, Summer immediately hung the phone up. She believed he wasn't like his brothers, but she had to cut all ties with him because she planned on killing his brother. If she had to, she wouldn't hesitate to kill him, as well.

Summer walked into the living room, picked up the folded bill with cocaine in it from the night before, and proceeded to sniff the remainder of the substance left. She then lay back on the couch and waited for the effects to take her mind adrift.

*   *   *   *   *

Two-Guns Paul and the twins, Porky & Biz, sat in a stolen jeep Durango watching Kevin and a couple of his boys from the cut.

"That's the nigga right there standing with that dyke bitch Judy." Porky pointed at Kevin and Judy who were getting in a double parked Escalade in front of their building. "Look like they're 'bout to pull off."

"Follow them."

*   *   *   *   *

"Come on, Judy, we got to make this move. Spyda is paging me." Kevin told everybody to be on point as he and Judy walked to the truck. "Here, Judy, you drive while I make these calls." Kevin threw Judy the keys to the Escalade.

160

The workers had just told Kevin that Bill Blast was arrested and talking about cooperating for less time. Kevin knew Bill Blast had some funny, weak shit with him, but he never thought he would go out like that. Kevin dialed Spyda's number while Judy pulled off.

"Hello."

"Yo, what's up?"

"Spyda, we just left from the building, and Tiny told me that Bill Blast got knocked and the nigga is talking about telling."

"Fuck that, nigga! He don't have anything to tell. Go to Underhill and move all of the drugs and guns."

"A'ight, me and Judy is on our way to handle that now."

"Ayo, send Tec and another soldier at that bitch he fucking with. Send that nigga a message that if he violated, his bitch can get it. What's that bitch's name?"

"Penny."

"Yeah, make sure they rough that lil' pretty bitch up and that he gets the message to keep his mouth shut."

"A'ight, Spyda, I'm on top of that. I'll see you when I leave Underhill. One!"

"A'ight!"

After Kevin hung up with Spyda, he called Tec and relayed the message about making a house call to Penny. As Judy pulled up to the light on Utica and Pacific, a car rear ended them.

"Oh shit, what the fuck was that?" Kevin hung the phone up as they both turned to see what hit them. Without thinking, Kevin jumped out of the truck and headed towards the Durango with tinted windows.

"Yo, what the fuck? Didn't you see the fucking light was red?" As Kevin approached the driver's side of the Durango, the passenger side and back doors swung open and Two-Guns and Porky jumped out with their pistols drawn, cocked back, and ready to air Kevin out if he made any sudden moves. Kevin froze with fear as he recognized Two-Guns Paul.

From the rearview mirror, Judy watched the men jump out, and as soon as she saw the guns, she pulled off.

"Don't move, muthafucka! If you say a word, you're dead." Two-Gun rushed Kevin and smacked him over the head with his pistol.

"Ugggh!" Kevin dropped to the ground. Two-Guns and his man grabbed Kevin up and threw him in the back seat of the car.

"Yo, let's go! Pull off!" Two-Gun told Biz as he pointed his heat at Kevin's head.

"Yo, Two-Guns, what's going on?" Kevin asked in a faint voice while holding his head.

"Nigga, shut the fuck up; you know what this is, nigga!"

* * * * *

"Cookie, where are you?"

"I'm with Capone. Why what's up?"

"You'll never believe what I just found out."

"What? What happened? Is everything alright?" Then it hit Cookie what it could be because she had just saw the news about Justin. "Summer, is this about the news?"

"Yes...so you know?"

"Yeah, your knight in shining armor is the brother of the people who killed your parents and the brother of Butter Bean."

"Cookie, I don't know what to believe right now. He tried to convince me that he wasn't like his family. I asked why he never told me this information, and he said because he knew it would affect our relationship and that he was afraid to lose me over the evils of his family."

"Listen, Summer, you got to stay focused. There's no room for mistakes right now if you want to get those responsible for your family's death, and Justin just might be your ticket. I think you can trust him."

"How can I trust somebody that's related to the people that murdered my parents?"

"Use him for what he's worth."

"I don't know, Cookie. Every time I think about him being related to the people who killed my mother and father, and possibly my sister and grandmother, hate builds up in my heart. That means he knew who I was the whole time, but tried to hide that info."

"Summer, have you heard the latest?"

"Nah, only what's been on the news."

"We might not have to worry about getting them because these fools is killing off each other. The reason I say I think you can trust Justin is because Butter sent some soldiers to rough Justin up, but Justin shot them both and then went to Butter's house and beat the shit out of him. Capone was also telling me that Big Ruben was murdered. These niggas is dropping like flies."

"Word!"

"Yeah, girl, and they think Butter and them had something to do with Justice."

"That's good. The best thing is that they will never expect anything because they have so much beef they won't know where it's coming from."

"Just be careful, Summer, and please don't make a move like you did last night. But right now, I'm waiting on Sha to come thru."

"You've been hanging with that chick a lot lately. What's up with Penny?"

"She had gone to the doctor's earlier. The bitch thinks she's pregnant."

"What? I still can't believe how y'all made this drastic change over night."

"Listen, Summer, as soon as I'm finished over here, I'ma come through."

"I'm about to head out. I can't stay up in this crib no longer. I'm going crazy. I need some air. But I'll be back around eleven or twelve."

"Come on, Summer, it's already nine-thirty. Where are you going?"

"I have something to do."

"What?"

"Bitch, I'm grown!"

"I just don't want you out there doing nothing crazy."

"Come on, Cookie, you don't have to worry about me."

"Just be careful, please!"

"Don't worry, Cookie."

After Summer hung up the phone, she got dressed, putting on the tightest, shortest, and most revealing skirt she could find. She put the gun she had taken from Justice in her Gucci bag, snatched her house keys up, and left. Heading for the old side of Smurf Village, she wanted to see what fish she could catch.

* * * * *

Justin lay on his couch thinking of Summer and how he hated what his family did, feeling as though he was being punished for their actions. Justin knew he should have told Summer, but how do you tell someone that your brothers were the ones who murdered their parents?

RING...RING...RING...

Mentally and physically exhausted, Justin took his time getting up off the couch to answer.

"Hello."

"Justin, the captain wants to see you in his office now."

"Alright, Kenneth, I'm on my way. Is everything alright?"

"Man, seems like he has an attitude. I told you he wanted to see you last night after the shooting."

"A'ight, I'm leaving the house right now."

"Bye!"

CLICK...

After hanging up, Justin put his gun in its holster and left the house. The one downside about homicide is you're on call 24/7. Justin knew the captain was going to chew his ass out and that this case was getting too much publicity. At this moment, Justin was operating on zero fuel. He hadn't been to bed in two nights, and for the last three months, these murders had been a lot on his plate and it wasn't until yesterday that they got any breaks. Bill Blast was willing to testify on Spyda about running the drugs, but he didn't know about any murders. He only had his speculations about Rashawn being murdered by Spyda, but had no accurate information. The other person they had ready to testify was Gutter. He said he could give up who was responsible for the deaths of Chuck and Hunt, plus he had the murder weapons. The only problem is he never said Butter was the leader; he pointed the finger at Dice. These two were the first breaks they got in the murders and war.

Justin got in the unmarked vehicle and pulled off.

*   *   *   *   *

After leaving the doctor's office, Penny went to her mother's house to get some motherly advice. The doctor calculated her to be six weeks pregnant, and Penny didn't know if she wanted to keep the child or not. She knew her mother would tell her the right thing to do. When Penny pulled up to the house, though, her mother's car wasn't parked out front.

"Oh, that's right. Ma started working the seven to three o'clock shift at the hospital now," Penny said to herself as she got out the car and walked to the door. When she reached into her bag to get the keys to her mother's door, she remembered Cookie came and got the keys the last night. Penny had Summer's keys and her mother's keys on the same keychain. "Damn!" As soon as Penny reached her car, her cell phone rang.

"Hello."

"Penny, it's me."

"Bill Blast, where are you? I thought you was coming over last night."

"I was on my way over there, but got locked up. I'm in jail."

"For what?"

"For gun possession."

"Do you have a bail?"

"Nah. I'm already a felon, so they won't give me bail. The feds is trying to pick up the case."

"What am I going to do now? I just left from seeing my doctor and I'm pregnant."

"Don't worry, ma. I'm working on something that's going to get me out of here. Where are you?"

"I'm headed back home."

"A'ight, I'ma call you back in an hour."

"A'ight, I should be home by then. Bye."

CLICK...

Chapter 13
Echoes Reveal
The Image Of Dreams

When Justin walked into the captain's office, Sergeant Walker and Kenneth were already there. Captain Staler, who had been on the force for the last twenty-two years, was a heavyset older black man with a salt and pepper beard and bald head. He smoked a pipe, so his office always stunk like tobacco smoke, that strong shit that choked non smokers when they smelled it.

"Hey! Look who finally decided to come join us?" Captain Staler pointed at Justin as he turned to Sergeant Walker. Justin entered and said nothing, simply acknowledging Walker and Kenneth with a head nod. Justin knew this couldn't be good. If just the sergeant was present, he could work with him, but the captain of the precinct was on another level.

"Listen, Detective Diekman, I'ma get right to the point. You are off this case and the streets for awhile," Captain Staler announced.

"Why? Why am I being demoted?" Justin asked with anger.

"Because when one of my officers is being threatened and thugs show up at their house, that tells me my officer's life is in danger. It's my responsibility to protect mines. So, you're off the streets."

"Nah, this is some bullshit!"

"If you keep that up, you will be suspended without pay. Diekman, how do you expect me to keep you on the streets after what happened last night? Furthermore, the feds are taking over the case. This thing is getting too much publicity. Word came down from the higher ups. This shit is bigger than what we think. We have an investigation underway, which involves your brother. Now how do you think that would look…a detective heading an investigation where his brother is one of the targets?"

"But, Captain, you know how I feel about my brothers. I'm the one who turned my other brothers in."

"Yeah, I know that and you know that, but what do you think the public is going to say? There are already allegations that your brother got the 77th under his payroll. So now we head an investigation with the suspect's brother? The media will chew us alive. Diekman, I have a precinct to run here. You go take a couple of days off to let your arm heal, and when you come back, this thing should have calmed down. I don't want you nowhere near this case. You hear me, Detective Diekman?"

"Yes, you're the boss." Justin turned with Kenneth behind him and left the office.

"Yo, Justin, wait up," Kenneth called out.

"What's up?" Justin walked to his desk to collect a few things.

"Man, Justin, this is for the best. You need a rest. I can see it in your eyes."

"Yeah, you're right, Kenneth. What they do to you?"

"They teamed me up with Barton, but we can't mess with the case. The feds is all over that."

"Damn! You stuck with that fool? At least you didn't get demoted."

"What 'cha about to do, Justin?"

"Nothing, maybe go to the bar and get my drink on."

"Man, it's only two o'clock in the afternoon."

"Yeah, but to me, I'm still going off of two days ago. I haven't been to bed yet."

"Hold on. I'ma roll with you."

"You're still on duty."

"No, I'm not. Hold up." Kenneth walked to his desk and collected a few things, as well. "Come on, I'm ready." Kenneth walked out of the precinct behind Justin.

* * * * *

Two-Guns Paul smacked and taunted Kevin in the backseat while Biz drove. Porky sat in the back, with Kevin squeezed in between them.

"Yo, bitch! Do you want to live or die? That's your call."

Kevin held his hands up to shield his face as he pleaded, "Come on, Two-Guns, you've known me for years. You know I ain't with the gangsta. I'm just a hustler."

"Yeah, but you fucking with them niggas who murdered my man Black Supreme." Two-Guns could smell the liquor on Kevin's breath. *This nigga stays getting drunk,* Two-Guns thought to himself as he backhanded Kevin in the mouth. "Put your muthafuckin' hands down, nigga! You making me nervous. You better tell me something. Where is that nigga Spyda?"

"Yo, Two-Guns, word is bond...I don't know. He don't tell me anything."

CRACK!

Kevin fell over on Porky. "Get your punk ass off of me." Porky pushed Kevin as he pointed his gun at Kevin's temple.

"Yo, Biz, ride to Evergreen Cemetery," Two-Guns called out. Biz shook his head in agreement.

"Please, Two-Guns, what are y'all going to do to me?"

"If you don't tell me something, your drunk ass won't live long enough to see. So, during this ride, you better think hard about what you going to tell us if you wanna walk away with your life." Two-Gun sat back, enjoying the fear he created. Something about being able to determine one's fate gave Two-Gun a God complex, and he liked it.

About fifteen minutes later, Biz pulled into the construction site behind the Evergreen Cemetery.

"Come on, get your ass out." Porky got out first and Kevin slowly exited the truck. Porky then led him to the back of the truck, opened the back, and sat him down. When Biz got out the truck with a gallon of gasoline in his hand, Kevin started panicking.

"Yo, please, man, don't kill me, please! My daughter is only two years old. Two-Gun, please!"

"Nigga, shut the fuck up and stop crying. You wasn't crying when you was running with them niggas from the old side getting that money. Kevin, I want to know something. Who killed Rashawn?"

"Yo, Two-Gun, I swear I don't know. Spyda running around saying that y'all killed him."

"Nigga, you know we didn't kill that nigga. Did Spyda set Rashawn up?"

"Two-Gun, I swear to God, man, they don't tell me nothing. The only reason that I'm somebody is because Big Ruben and Justice were murdered. Other than that, I'm just a hustler."

"Listen, Kevin, do you think this nigga Spyda is worth your life? That nigga don't give a fuck about you. You better tell me something, or I'm going to let my man pour that gasoline on that ass and light it." Two-Gun looked at Biz and gave him a head nod. Biz poured some of the gasoline over Kevin and lit a match.

"Two-Gun, please! No! Hold up, hold up! I'll tell you where the stash spot is at."

"Hold up, Biz." Two-Gun stopped Biz as he walked towards Kevin with the lit match.

"You better tell us something, nigga. Where that nigga live?"

"I don't know where he lives. All I know is that he moved to Queens with his baby's mother, Linda, but the stash house is on Dean and Underhill, the corner gray building, apartment 3a. That's where they stash the money, guns, and drugs."

"What else do you have that's worth saving your life?"

"He knows that Sha is fucking with Butter, and he thinks she set up Big Ruben and Justice, so he plans on killing her tonight. Now, please, that's all I have."

"Oh yeah! Is that so?"

Bung...Bung...Bung!

Kevin's body collapsed to the ground. As Biz and Porky picked his body up and tossed it in the truck, Two-Gun shouted, "Blaze that muthafucka!"

Porky poured the rest of the gasoline all over the Durango, and then Biz threw the match on Kevin's body. As the car went up in smoke Two-Guns Paul, Porky, and Biz took off running.

*　*　*　*　*

Beast, Ace, and Shorty were all in front of the building watching the workers make sales. Beast and the crew were praying that somebody jumped out of line tonight. Even if a nigga came through driving and reckless eyeballing, he would get it. Everybody was on edge and jumpy. Ace was a trigger happy lil nigga that didn't give a fuck about nothing but getting a name for himself as a killer. They actually felt somewhat sorry for anybody that came through tonight, especially the boys in blue from the 71st who was working for the Bloods. They had enough guns out tonight to fight off a precinct. When Two-Guns Paul told them to be ready for anything and to be on point, it meant for them to strap up with the heavy metal.

"Yo, Cipher!" one of the lookouts called out as a patrol car slowly passed by. They stared at first, but kept riding pass as the pitchers continued to serve the fiends. All the gunmen grabbed hold of their heat just in case the police wanted to act stupid, but they just turned their heads and kept it moving as if they didn't see anything. If it had been the 71st, things might have gone down a little different.

"Yo, don't worry. It's just the 77th. They're not worrying about us because most of them is on the payroll,"

Bloody Dog said as he laughed and turned his attention back to the light bright shorty he was talking to.

Although shit was hot, the money continued to come at a rapid pace. The only thing the heads feared was not being able to get some more rock. Another reason the drug traffic was so deep during the war time was because Butter told the workers to cut throat and sell what everybody else sold for five dollars for just three dollars. Three dollar bumps had the heads coming all day. So, Beast had everybody out pushing three dollar bumps since the spot got shut down.

Beast just turned twenty-three, and Butter had placed him in charge of the pitchers; he was also responsible for the hiring of the workers. Beast made sure he recruited fourteen to sixteen-year-olds to sell the drugs and hold down the workers. Most of Beast's workers were still in junior high school. They were easier to please because all you had to give them was a new pair of sneakers, a gold chain, and some weed to smoke. All of his workers were from the new side and their parents were either smoked out or in jail, so they took care of themselves. Beast paid all his workers with product, so when they finished Butter's shit, they were allowed to hustle their shit.

Beast got his name from his ruthlessness and harsh looks. He was charcoal black with a hairy face and 250 pounds of pure muscles. Beast had a face only a mother could love, and his attitude matched his looks. He never had a steady girlfriend because women were scared of him. The only real relationships Beast ever had with women was with the crackhead bitches he tricked with frequently, and his arrangement with women was fine with him. When he paid for pussy, there were no attachments involved…just hit 'em and go. When crack hit the market, he was able to fuck all types of women.

For the first time, a shorty walking pass had stopped Beast in his track. First of all, no bad shorties ever walked through their projects this late. Beast looked at her as she walked towards him. She was slim and light skin just the way he liked them. Shorty wore the most revealing dress he had ever seen, showing all thighs, and as she walked by, it was if her ass cheeks were calling his name. Beast's manhood immediately stood at attention. He had to have her and couldn't contain himself. Beast did something he hardly ever did; he grabbed the girl by her arm to try to stop her from walking pass him.

Summer stopped and snatched her arm from Beast. Already knowing who he was, she turned around and said, "Excuse me, but do you fucking know me to be grabbing on my arm?"

"I'm sorry, ma, but I was just trying to get your attention."

"That's not how you do it." Summer rolled her eyes, but did not want to overplay it.

"I apologize, ma. What's your name?" Beast asked with confidence.

Looking at his face, Summer immediately knew why they called him Beast.

"My name is Porsche, but you can call me Beauty so we can be beauty and the beast," Summer replied in a flirtatious manner.

Her response caught Beast off guard, and he found himself blushing. "Umm, beauty and the beast sounds good to me. How can we hook up?"

"You can give me your number and I'll call you in about an hour. Right now, I'm in a rush and don't feel comfortable talking to you with all of your boys around. Another thing, these projects have been off the hook lately. I don't wanna get shot while just standing and talking to you."

Beast wrote his number on a matchbook cover he had in his pocket and passed it to Summer. "Page me in an hour; I should be done with what I'm doing by then. A'ight?"

"A'ight, Beast, one hour. You best not have me waiting by a payphone and you don't call me right back. I'm not playing. Don't have me waiting, or you will see who the real beast is." Summer smiled as she stuck the number in her bag, making sure she didn't open it too much where he would see the gun inside.

"Nah, ma, don't worry about that. A nigga is feeling you. I'ma definitely call your fine self right back."

As he watched her walk off, he wanted to call her back and drive her wherever she wanted to go, but knew he had to handle business. Besides, he didn't want to look too thirsty, but he couldn't wait for her to call.

* * * * *

An hour later, Beast's pager went off.

"Yeah, boy! That's that fine ass shorty I just pulled." Beast looked at his pager as he hit Ace on the arm. "Yo, son, let me use your cell phone real quick."

"Say word, son! That fine ass chick is calling your ugly ass back?" Ace burst into laughter as Beast gave him a look as if to say, *Nigga, don't play.*

"Yo, dawg, that bitch looks real familiar. I know her from some place, but don't know just where yet," Shorty said.

"Ah, you niggas need to stop hating on the Blood because a nigga pulled a hottie." Beast turned his back to Ace and Shorty as he dialed the number. "Hello, did somebody page this number?"

"Hey, Beast, it's Porsche."

"Oh, what's up, baby girl? What 'cha doing?"

"I'm over at my cousin's house. Will you come and pick me up."

"Where you at?"

"In Albany projects...the Troy Avenue side."

"Word! A'ight, be downstairs because I don't be going up in nobody else's projects."

"A'ight, I'll be downstairs waiting outside."

Beast passed the cell phone back to Ace and gave them both dap. "Yo, y'all hold the soldiers down. I'll be right back. If Two-Guns, Dice, or any of them niggas come looking for me, tell 'em I went to the crib to put up some of this money, ya heard?"

"A'ight, Blood, hit them draws for me, too."

"Man, for all of us," Shorty responded.

"No doubt. One!" Beast peeled off from the crew in a hurry in his Ford Explorer.

Chapter 14
Drop 'Em One By One

Judy ran by the group of teenagers standing in front of the building smoking a blunt and up the stairs to Ms. Price's apartment. Ms. Price was a crackhead who allowed Spyda to use her apartment as a stash house and the hangout for the soldiers. Ms. Price had three daughters who were all in their early 20's. The whole crew had run through all of them, even Judy. The girls were all nice looking, but they just had that project chickenhead mentality. Ms. Price was a dope fiend turned crackhead, and Spyda and the boys took care of the entire family.

Ms. Price's oldest daughter, Nia, was tall and built like a horse, plenty of ass but a horrible face. She had these dick-sucking lips, but the bad part about it was she didn't know how to suck good head. She was perfect when it came to boosting clothes, though. That was her specialty. Nia was the spitting image of her father, a drunk who always hung out on the corner. Ms. Price's youngest daughter, Niema, looked like her mother. By looking at her, you could tell Ms. Price was right before she became strung out on drugs. Niema worked for Spyda, cook and bagging up the work. Egypt, the middle child, was about her business and the best out of the bunch. She didn't look like none of her sisters or her mother; you could tell she had a different father from the rest of them. As a matter of fact, all three sisters had different fathers, but Egypt's father was a white man who was one of Ms. Price's tricks back in her whoring days. Egypt was different from her sisters; she felt if a nigga wanted what she had between her legs, they would have to pay and pay good money. Egypt wasn't trying to fuck for free like her sisters, and niggas were willing to pay for Egypt because she was the shit in the projects. Judy tricked big money on Egypt. Egypt was golden brown with long, straight, black hair, and gray eyes. Ms. Judy always told her that she favored her father, who Egypt never met. This was one of the reasons she hated white people and the main reason she used men only for their money.

When Judy ran in the house, Ms. Price and the girls were sitting in the kitchen, while a couple of the soldiers were sitting on the couch playing video games and smoking weed.

"Yo, they just snatched up Kevin!" Judy was out of breath and apparently shaken.

"What?!" Jimbo asked as he jumped up.

"They just snatched up Kevin!"

"Who?"

"The muthafuckas from the old side. I think it was that lil' nigga Two-Guns Paul and the twins, but I didn't get a good look at their faces, so I'm not sure." Judy went to the back to use the phone, and they all followed behind her.

"What the fuck happened?"

"We was headed to Underhill and a car crashed into the back of us. Kevin got out beefing with the drivers of the Durango. I was watching from the rearview mirror when I saw muthafuckas jumping out with guns. That's when I pulled off." Judy dialed the number and motioned for the blunt while she waited for Spyda to pick up.

* * * * *

Spyda laid next to Linda with Sha on his mind. His only reason for being with Linda is because he felt obligated to take care of her and the kids, but his feelings for her had been long gone. Linda went down on him while his mind wondered elsewhere. Linda didn't even turn him on anymore; not even her famous dick sucking abilities did anything for him.

Spyda was sick about Sha. He had sent the word for her to be dealt with and felt at this moment he was losing the war. The worst part was that people actually believed he had something to do with his man's death. Butter and his crew of Bloods were getting the best of him. They killed Big Ruben, Justice, and now the bitch he had chose over his baby's mother was snaking behind his back fucking with the enemy, not to mention the nigga Bill Blast telling it all. Spyda contemplated just making a move, fuck it all before it was too late. Fuck the Pj's, the court case, Linda and the kids, everything…and just bounce before it was too late. As far as Linda was concerned, he had a feeling she was cheating on him, but at this point, he didn't even care as long as she didn't bother him.

"Spyda, what's wrong?" Linda raised her head from between his legs as she continued to jerk his manhood. "You not feeling me tonight? I've been trying to get you excited for about thirty minutes now. Usually, as soon as my lips touch the head, it's standing at attention."

"Man, I'm going through it right now. They killed my boys Ruben and Justice."

"What!" Linda stood up in surprise.

Spyda looked at Linda. Seeing the hurt and concern in her eyes, he knew right then who Linda was fucking.

"Why the fuck you acting like you so hurt about Ruben and Justice? You didn't even like them."

Linda simply lowered her head.

"Bitch, was you fucking my mans and them?"

"Spyda, why would you ask me something so crazy? Anyway, what if I was? You don't fuck me no more. You too busy fucking that bitch Sha. Your dick don't even get hard from me sucking on your dick no more." Linda got up out of the bed and left the room.

Spyda knew she had fucked either Big Ruben or Justice, and he bet it was Lil' Justice because that lil' nigga was shiesty like that. *Big Ruben would never do some shit like that. He had too much loyalty,* Spyda thought to himself as he laid on the bed and his thoughts drifted back to Sha.

RING...RING...RING...

Spyda's thoughts were interrupted by the phone and he knew Linda's ass wasn't going to answer it because she was upset. Therefore, Spyda reached over and grabbed the phone off of its base.

"Hello."

"Spyda!"

Spyda sat up and looked at the clock. It was only after nine, but it felt much later. "Yeah, what's up?"

"This is Judy. Them niggas from the old side just snatched up Kevin!"

"What?"

"I think it was Two-Guns and the twins."

"Yo, tell everybody to meet me at Underhill."

"A'ight."

CLICK...

"Muthafucka!" Spyda screamed as he got out of bed. "I'ma kill these niggas tonight!"

Spyda went into his wallet and pulled out Dollar Bill's number. Spyda told Dollar Bill that he had a job for him. "It concerns that nigga Butter." Dollar Bill automatically knew what Spyda wanted, and told him that he would get on top of that as soon as possible.

After Spyda hung the phone up, he got dressed and left the crib.

* * * * *

Beast waited in front of the building Summer told him that she was at. He had already been sitting and waiting for over twenty minutes. The one thing everybody knew is that you don't go into another person's project, especially for a bitch, because most of the time it's a set up. But Beast was so open on the fact that someone as good looking as Summer got back at him, he didn't realize what he was doing. Beast started getting impatient and realized he was committing the number one thing on his list of "Things Not to Do to Survive in the Streets". However, Beast figured since he was holding, fuck it! Whatever. If one of these clowns got out of hand, he would let them have it. Besides, he was Blood and the majority of Albany projects were Damu.

Just as he was about to pull off, his pager sounded. Beast recognized the number as the same number Summer had called from earlier. Beast smiled to himself as he looked up and noticed the payphone on the corner in front of a building that looked abandoned. He tucked the hammer in his waist and exited the truck. He had heard the rep that

Albany projects had, but this night, you could hear a pin drop. The only thing moving was a few crackheads going in and out of the spot across the street from the Pj's. Outside of that, the only motion was the #65 bus pulled over at the bus stop on the corner. He constantly looked over his shoulders as he dialed the number. An answering machine recording came on... *"Please leave a message at the sound of the beep...BEEP!"*

Man, what the fuck! Beast thought to himself, frustrated that he wasn't able to get through. He hung the phone up and dialed once again, but this time, the phone just constantly rang. "Man, what type of fucking games is this bitch playing?" Beast slammed the phone down.

"Hey!"

Beast jumped as he reached into his waist, pulled out his shit, spun around, and pointed. A basehead lady that looked on the edge of death was startled by the sight of the gun in Beast's hand.

"What the fuck is your crackhead doing creeping up on me for, bitch?"

After the lady stopped shaking, she got up the nerve to ask Beast what she had approached him for. "Excuse me, but can you spare a dollar?"

"Nah, bitch! I don't have shit. Now get the fuck away from me. You lucky I didn't shoot your stinking ass." As he put his weapon back in his waist, he turned and started walking back towards his truck.

"Beast!"

Recognizing the voice, Beast stopped and turned around in the middle of the street. Summer exited the abandoned looking building. The first thing that came to Beast's mind was what the fuck was Summer doing coming out of the abandoned building, but he just figured she was

183

hustling. Unbeknownst to Beast, Summer had the 9mm cocked behind her back as she walked towards him.

"Damn, ma, you had a brother in these Pj's looking crazy. I almost just killed a muthafucka." Beast started walking back towards the sidewalk to meet Summer. As he got closer, Summer pulled the gun from behind her back and pointed it at Beast. Beast froze, "Yo, ma, what the fuck is this?"

"Muthafucka, the word on the streets is that y'all 'niggas is responsible for my sister's death."

"Ma, I don't even know who your sistah is."

"Yes, you do muthafucka…Destiny!"

Beast thought about the name and then it hit him. "Yo, we didn't have nothing to do with that shit."

Beast thought he could pull his gat before she made a move, having sized her up and figuring her not being able to shoot. He flinched, but before he could react, the deafening sounds of gunfire echoed through the quiet night. The slugs hit Beast's body as if he was hit by a sledgehammer. The impact of each slug tore into Beast's body and threw him back into the middle of the street. Summer continued to hold the trigger until the gun was empty before she ran off.

Beast was dead before he hit the ground.

*   *   *   *   *

Butter lay in the bed with Passion in his arms. He had been fucking Passion all day. She was on cloud nine and quickly slipping into the point of no return. Butter and Dice had schooled Passion on what to do and how to do it when the time was right for her to kill Justin. In between Butter schooling her on how to kill and get away with it, he fucked her young brains out. Passion was beyond being in love with Butter; she worshipped him and was willing to give up her own life force so he would be able to live if she had to.

"Daddy, do you really love me like you say you do? Do I really make you feel like no other woman makes you feel?" Passion asked as she laid her head on Butter's chest and he rubbed on her ass. Butter palmed both ass cheeks in his hands and gave a firm squeeze.

"Come on, ma, you my girl. Not just my fuck kitten, but my main girl now. It's about you and me. That's why I cut everybody off. It's all about you, girl."

"What about Sha?"

"Sha is history, ma. She don't have nothing on my Passion. I'ma make you wifey." Butter was telling Passion everything she wanted to hear, and she was taking it all in, getting her hopes up all high. "Ma, after tonight, I want you to leave home and come stay with me. This is your new home."

"What about my parents? They're not just going to let me up and leave." Passion sat up and stared into Butter's eyes.

"Ma, I'm your parent. I'm your father and you're my mother. It's about you and me." Passion smiled from ear to ear as the words Butter was kicking went straight to her heart. She then started licking and sucking down Butter's chest until she reached his manhood. Passion kissed the head of his cock, then took him into her mouth and proceeded to do what she loved to do.

Butter's cell phone started vibrating. He held Passion's head with one hand and with the free hand, he answered the call. "Two?"

"Yeah, we got the nigga; he's Elvis. And we got the address to the stash house."

"A'ight. I'm in the middle of something right now, but give me a holla in about a half." Butter knew Two-Guns could hear the slurping sounds Passion made with his dick, and he tried hard to suppress his moan from her deep throat action.

"Yo, Butter, what the fuck? You getting your man ate?" Two-Guns Paul asked as he started laughing. "A'ight, son, but yo, them niggas is also planning on killing Sha. They know she set Big Ruben up and they think we killed Justice. So tell her to stay away from them niggas."

"A'ight. One!" Butter hurried up and hung up the phone. He couldn't really think about what Two-Guns was talking about. Passion had him on another plane. Butter closed his cell phone, grabbed Passion's head with both hands, and started fucking her mouth.

* * * * *

Justin had been at the bar ever since he left the precinct that afternoon. It was already after nine o'clock, and he was still getting drunk. Kenneth had left about an hour ago, but Justin stayed. He continued to order drinks to his corner booth off by himself as he tried to drown his anger and disappointment over the whole situation surrounding his family and him losing Summer. He was determined to drink his stress away tonight. He was willing to deal with them tomorrow, but for today, he preferred to drink and soak in his guilt.

Little did Justin know, he was being watched. Bloody Dog had entered the bar about an hour ago to serve a fiend and noticed Justin in the corner getting bent by his himself. After about an hour of watching him, Bloody Dog left and called Butter.

*　*　*　*　*

When Spyda pulled into the block and parked in front of the building on Underhill, agents seated in a dark-colored sedan across the street from the building watched. "There goes our main target right there getting out of the Escalade." The head agent pointed at Spyda as he spoke on his walkie talkie to the other agents already stationed in the building.

The agent turned as he looked at the other agents in the car with him. "Is everybody ready? Remember, these are the people who are responsible for the rising death toll in our streets, so be careful."

All the agents checked their weapons and waited for the head agent to give the word. As soon as Spyda entered the building, the head agent told the other agents over the radios to wait until they moved in to make a move. Then the agents in the car got out and ran to the building.

When Spyda opened the door, Judy, Niema, Jimbo and a couple other soldiers and workers were all sitting in the front room. Before Spyda could close the door behind him, the agents came rushing in.

"Freeze! Don't move! FBI!"

Before Spyda could react, he was slammed to the floor and handcuffed. Several other agents ran pass him, and then he heard gunfire erupt in the back. As about ten more agents ran towards the back, Spyda looked at Judy as if questioning her on who was in the back room.

Judy whispered, "Tiny and Dave."

Spyda just closed his eyes and shook his head.

* * * * *

"Yes, daddy, shove that big dick in my tight ass!" Passion screamed as Butter penetrated her from behind. Passion tried her best to sound grown and provocative, but with everything she said, you could tell she was young. Still, that didn't stop Butter. He knew he had something young and dumb that was willing to kill for him.

"Yeah, mommy, this ass feels just as good as that tight pussy of yours. I think I'm in love!" Butter played on Passion's young mind, stroking her emotions.

"Yes, daddy, I'm yours to do with whatever you want." The more Passion moaned and grunted, the harder Butter would fuck her. He had his manhood all the way in her virgin anal canal. Passion screamed from the pain, but the pleasure of knowing she was pleasing Butter made the pain bearable. Passion laid on her stomach as Butter rode her. "Oh God! Ride this ass, daddy!"

Butter plunged deeper until he was inside of her up to the hilt of his manhood. Passion played with herself, bringing herself to an orgasm as she took Butter's entire dick in her ass.

"Come on, daddy, let's change positions." Butter pulled his dick out of her ass and turned Passion on her back, raising her legs over his shoulders. "Daddy, put it back in my ass." Passion continued to rub her clit; she tensed up as Butter rammed his massive cock back in her ass.

I love this lil' bitch, Butter thought as he roughly fucked Passion, giving her what she wanted.

"Oh, daddy, I love you! Please don't ever stop!" Passion cried out as she looked into Butter's eyes and the

188

tears started to flow. Passion couldn't believe how much she loved this man. She prayed he would never leave her. At only sixteen, she was willing to give everything up for this man she thought she loved. "Oh my god! Yes!" Passion moaned as she felt Butter's hot cum fill her insides.

"Lil Ma, did you like that?" Butter asked as he turned over and reached for the half of blunt in the ashtray.

"Daddy, I love pleasing my man. If it pleases you, I like it."

Butter ran his hand through Passion's hair. "Here, ma, puff on this with me." He passed her the blunt while he got up and went into the bathroom.

When Butter exited the bathroom, Passion was sitting up in the bed. She had rolled another blunt and passed Butter his cell phone, which had gone off while he was in the bathroom. She knew better than to answer it. "Here, daddy, it's been going off like crazy."

"Thanks, ma," Butter sat on the edge of the bed and answered the phone. "Yo!"

"Butter, guess what? That nigga Justin is at the bar right now drunk as fuck. I can get the nigga now," Bloody Dog said in an excited tone.

"Nah, son, I don't need y'all doing nothing. I'ma send somebody else. What bar?"

"The joint on Utica and St. Marks."

"Yo, when he leaves, call me."

"A'ight."

"One!" When Butter hung up, he called Dice.

"Hello."

"Dice, it's on and poppin'. That nigga Bloody Dog just called and told me that Justin is at the bar drunk as fuck. It's time for that nigga to pay for what he did to me and our older brothers. It's time for him to answer for his punk ass daddy, as well."

"Butter, I'll be right over."

"Hurry up." Butter hung up and turned to Passion. "Now, are you ready to make good on what you promised me?"

Passion knew exactly what Butter was talking about. "Yes, daddy, anything to make you happy."

"That's what I'm talking about, ma, but right now, I want to make you happy before it goes down." Butter motioned for Passion to lay on her back as he spread her legs apart and positioned his mouth over her womanhood. Her pussy throbbed for his touch, and as soon as his tongue came in contact with her hotness, she quivered. Passion felt his hot tongue tapping against her clit which sent immediate surges of pleasure throughout her entire body. She grabbed hold of Butter's head as he went to work. All she could think about was how she would do anything for this man. After only three minutes of Butter working his powerful tongue, Passion was cumming.

Chapter 15
It's Always The Ones Closest To You

As Penny was returning from her mother's house, she noticed Summer walking at a fast pace and with a distraught look on her face, as if she had seen a ghost.

"Summer," Penny called out to her as she rolled down her window.

Summer looked up quickly, and then ran over to the car. "What's up, girl?"

"Where were you on your way to in such a hurry?"

"Where do you think I was going headed in this direction? I was on my way to your house." Summer jumped into Penny's car. "Where you on your way to?"

"Girl! I had the most stressful day. I found out that I'm pregnant."

"Get the fuck out of here! By who?" Summer asked as she leaned over to turn down Penny's radio.

"Girl, you don't know him. He's a new piece of thang thang that I've been creeping with. I met him a couple of months ago," Penny responded, refusing to tell Summer that she was pregnant by Bill Blast. "Anyway, I went to my mother's house to tell her, but I forgot I had her keys on the same keychain I had yours on, which I gave to Cookie because she had left her keys at your house and you wasn't answering the phone. Anyway, when I get home, I get a collect call from my soon-to-be baby's father, who got locked up the night before, so I'm just coming from the jail. That shit alone is another situation in itself." Penny shook her head as if she was exhausted. "So now, I'm pregnant and my baby's daddy is facing how much time I can't begin to tell you." Penny brushed her bangs out of her face while navigating her car through traffic.

"Girl, you done stressed me out worse than what I already am. Where's the get high at? I know you have a stash somewhere."

"There's half of a blunt in there." Penny pointed at the ashtray.

"Come on, girl! I know you have something stronger than that."

Penny looked at Summer and automatically knew what she was talking about. "Oh, you're talking about *that*, huh? Look in my purse. There should be at least a half gram left. Girl, don't tell me that you're hooked on the shit already."

"Nah, I'm just so stressed out. These dreams are getting worse. It's as if Destiny is trying to tell me something. Lately, there has been an image of a girl in my dreams. Sometimes it's so intense it seems like I'm witnessing the murders...like my dreams are trying to reveal who's behind the murders. The only thing is I can't make out the face of the girl in my dreams." Summer took the lil' baggy out of Penny's purse and used her pinky nail to scoop the cocaine as she sniffed.

"This shit is really bothering me, but I know everything is going to come to light real soon. I was watching the news and found out Justin, the detective I was telling you about, is the brother of the people who killed my parents, and he is also Butter Bean's brother. So I told him that I don't ever want to see him again. I don't know if I did the right thing, though. This shit got me so stressed out. All I have is you and Cookie. And if anything ever happened to y'all, I'd be no more good."

Sniff, Sniff...

Penny looked at her best friend and figured now was the time. She pulled her car over and parked it in front of a school. "Summer, I have something to tell you, but I don't know how. I've wanted to tell you for a while now, but I had to make sure first."

Summer lifted her head and wiped the cocaine residue from her nose. "Penny, you know you can tell me anything, sis."

"It's about who killed Destiny and Ms. Hardy."

"What?" Summer turned her attention to Penny. "What are you talking about?"

"I think I know who killed Destiny and Ms. Hardy." Penny looked into Summer's eyes, which displayed nothing but hatred from the mentioning of the murder of her family.

"What, Penny? Don't play with me. What do you know?"

Penny dropped her head.

"Penny, you better tell me something. Who killed my sister?"

Penny looked at Summer with tears in her eyes and took a deep breath.

"Summer, what I'm about to tell you I'm not sure of, but it's something I heard with my own two ears. I think Cookie had something to do with the murders."

"What?! Where did you hear that from?"

"I overheard a conversation that Cookie was having over the phone with a familiar voice which sounded like that nigga Spyda."

"What'd you hear?"

"One day after the murders, I picked up the phone to use it and Cookie was on the line. I played like I hung up, but I was still on the phone. To this day, she doesn't know I heard the conversation. Summer, Cookie and Spyda had set Rashawn up, and when they went to kill him, Destiny was there and saw their faces, so they killed her and your grandmother."

"Penny, why'd you never tell me this?"

"I didn't know what to believe. I was fucked up about you, and then when you came out the hospital, I didn't know how to tell you. Summer, you know how I felt about your grandmother and Destiny. Y'all were my family, as well. And you know Cookie is my blood. We were raised together, so I was torn. But right is right and wrong is wrong. I feel bad, and the guilt of what my blood did is killing me. I can't sleep at night knowing what I know. I feel Cookie should pay for what she did." Penny paused before continuing, trying to read the expression on Summer's face. "I know it's hard to believe, but it's true. I wouldn't lie to you about this. Once a month, Spyda blessed Cookie with a lump sum of money. That's how her man Capone got on. But he doesn't know about what she did. He thinks she got the money from a lawsuit she won."

Summer just stared out the window and remained speechless. The first thing that went through Summer's mind was her latest dreams and the image of the girl. Was it of Cookie? Summer placed both hands over her face as she started crying.

"Summer, are you alright?"

"No! Hell fucking no! I'm just finding out that my best friend, who I looked at like a sister, had something to do with my sister's death." Summer picked her head up and looked at Penny. "You know I'm going to murder her, right?"

Penny put her head down. "I know, and I think she needs to pay for what she did. I just didn't feel right keeping it from you; I had to tell you. Summer, you are a sister to me, and there's no forgiving what Cookie has done. One of the reasons I started using drugs and drinking is to cope with what I heard. I hope you can forgive me for not telling you, but I just couldn't bring myself to tell you any sooner. But the burden became too much for me."

Penny leaned over and hugged Summer as they both cried. Summer cried knowing that she was going to have to kill her best friend, and Penny cried from the guilt of her own actions.

Penny dropped Summer off at home, then pulled off. As soon as she turned the corner, Penny pulled out her cell phone and made a call.

"It's Penny. I just told her exactly what you told me to tell her."

"A'ight, ma, that's good. I'ma creep by later on tonight to see you. You did good. Don't worry. Everything is going to be okay."

"I hope so. Bye."

CLICK...

* * * * *

Dice and Passion sat across the street from the bar waiting for Justin to leave so they could follow him. When Bloody Dog called Butter back and told him that Justin was about to leave, Dice and Passion were already in route to the bar. On the drive there, Dice continued to drill how important it was for Passion to do what she had to do and get out in a hurry. They had abandoned their first plan of Passion playing like she murdered Justin in self defense because he was drunk and tried to rape her. They decided it would be best for her to do what she had to do and get the fuck in the wind.

"Passion, are you ready?" Dice asked as he passed her the .380 caliber handgun.

"Yeah, I'm ready to get him for what he did to you, daddy," Passion replied with a serious look of determination in her eyes. Dice looked in Passion's face and only then noticed she was just a kid that thought she was in love with Mr. Right. Dice felt somewhat sorry for her.

"Remember, Passion, once you get out this car, you're on your own. If you're having second thoughts let me know now, because once you're out there is no turning back." Something in Dice wanted to try to persuade her not to do it.

"I know, Dice; I can and want to do this for you, daddy."

"A'ight then, heads up! Justin just walked out the bar and is headed for his car." Dice pointed at Justin who was staggering to his car. "That nigga is drunk as hell. You might not have to do anything. If we're lucky, that muthafucka will crash and kill his own ass."

As they watched Justin get in his car and pull off, Dice pulled off behind him.

*   *   *   *   *

As soon as Dice and Passion left the house, Butter decided to call Sha. She had been on his mind, plus he wanted to let her know not to go around Spyda and the others because they knew she had set Big Ruben up. Not to mention, he was in the mood for some of her good pussy. He hadn't been with Sha in over a week and she had him fiending for her sex. Before he could pick the phone up, though, it started ringing.

"Goddamn! What the fuck!" Butter looked at the caller ID and recognized the number. "Yo."

"Butter, this is Two-Guns. Me and the twins is at the Pj's."

"What's poppin'?"

"Shit is hectic; the feds is running up in the Pj's as we speak. We over here at D-Brown's crib across the street. I just saw them put Ace, Lil' Murder, Shorty, and Bloody Dog in the van. And yo, they found Beast dead in the Albany projects last night. The lil' homies from that end was telling me this when I stopped by the weed gate on Fulton."

"What? Get the fuck out of here! Who was he going to see in the Albany projects? And I just got off the phone with Bloody Dog about twenty minutes ago."

"Yeah, well, the feds rushed the building. I don't know who else or what they caught. Shit is crazy. The feds is swarming the building. We watching the shit go down."

"Yo, y'all niggas stay put and call me when shit clears. I'ma call Dice and tell him not to go over there."

"A'ight, dog, we'll hit you back later."

"One!"

After Butter hung up with Two-Guns, he paged Dice and then called Sha.

* * * * *

"Yeah, Cookie, just tell your girl Summer I'ma hook up with her at another time. I hope she don't think I'm trying to avoid her or nothing, but you know the deal."

"I'll let her know. I don't think she feels like you're putting her off, but I'm just nervous. Shit got out of hand, and it feels like I'm stuck in the middle. Summer is my girl, and I want whoever is responsible for Destiny and Ms. Hardy's deaths just as bad as she does."

Sha looked at Cookie, and at that point, Sha realized Cookie didn't have a clue as to what was going on. "Girl, don't even stress that. You know everything in the dark eventually comes to light. Whoever is responsible, the streets will reveal in due time." Sha lit her Newport and inhaled. "Yeah, I want who's responsible myself, and I got a pretty good idea who it is."

At first, Sha was naive to what was going on, but now that she was filled in, she knew Cookie wasn't accountable for the murders. Since she wasn't, who was? Sha offered Cookie a cigarette, which she accepted.

"The reason I'm so worried about my girl is because she's on some real vigilante type shit and out for justice. I'm afraid she's going to get hurt, locked up, or even killed. A lot of innocent people might die," Cookie said as she inhaled the smoke.

"Yeah, but are they truly innocent? The answer will come out soon…trust, Cookie. You and your girl just remain patient."

BUZZZ…BUZZZ…BUZZZ…

Sha pulled her BlackBerry off her hip and looked at the screen. "And that's my cue to be out." Sha smiled as she read the message Butter had sent. "Cookie, I'll get back at you tomorrow. Tell my brother when he comes out the shower that I'll call him later."

"A'ight, girl, will do." Cookie gave Sha a hug before she left. Afterwards, Cookie went into the kitchen and made herself a grilled cheese sandwich while she waited for Capone to drop her off at Summer's house.

* * * * *

"Listen, we have three people willing to testify against you, a house full of drugs and guns, and another two people saying you gave the word to murder. I don't know what type of crew you think you had, but they all are willing to make deals to save their asses. The only real friends you had were the ones that decided they could shoot their way out of the house, and you see where that got them. Both of them are dead. You are the only one that can help you right now. So what is it going to be? Do you know what 848 is? That alone can put you away for life," the frail agent whose breath smelled like coffee and cheese asked as he sat across from Spyda and stared at him with his shades on.

"What can y'all do for me?" Spyda asked nervously, knowing his life was in their hands.

"It's not what we can do for you; it's what you can do for yourself."

"Is the U.S Attorney willing to give me full pardon?"

"That depends on what you have for us."

"How about I give y'all three bodies that include a sixteen-year-old and her grandmother? As a bonus, I'll throw in a list of corrupt cops."

"Are you talking about the Hardy case?"

"Yes."

"Then continue," the agent said with excitement.

"I will when I find out if the U.S Attorney is willing to play ball." Spyda sat back; he knew he had the ball in his court. This was a high profile case, and they were getting pressured to solve it. Before leaving the room, the agent smiled and told Spyda that he would get back at him.

* * * * *

As Summer sat on the couch waiting for Cookie, the hatred within built up beyond her comprehension. Summer knew she had to calm down and not let her emotions supersede her intelligence. Cookie had to die for her betrayal, but how was the question. The gun Summer took from Justice had no more bullets and she knew she couldn't kill Cookie in the house, but if she saw Cookie right then, nothing would be able to stop her from killing her with her bare hands, which would not be a wise move.

Summer wanted to be able to walk away knowing she would not have to serve life in jail for somebody as low as Cookie. She couldn't believe Cookie had smiled in her face and slept in Destiny's bed knowing she had killed her. Summer wanted her to suffer. For every day Summer refused to shed a tear for her situation, Cookie would have to pay five times the suffering, resulting in her own death.

Summer checked the gun she used to kill Beast with and noticed she had no more bullets. "Shit! Where the fuck am I going to get more bullets from?" The first name that came to her mind was Justin. So, she decided to go visit him. Besides, she wanted to see him anyway. She no longer blamed him for what his brothers did. How could she when as of a few days ago she had become a worse animal than they were. With the visit, she would be able to get some bullets *and* satisfy the itch in her pants. Yes, that would be the plan. She would fuck the shit out of him. Then when he fell off to sleep, she would steal a case of bullets, go kill Cookie, and then return to the house before he got up. He would be her alibi.

Summer hurried and left the house before Cookie showed up.

Chapter 16
Death For Betrayal

Detective Samson laid next to Jenny, the hooker he just finished fucking. He met Jenny about a month ago when he arrested her during a raid on a crack house. Jenny propositioned him with sex if he let her go, and Samson agreed. He has been fucking her every Saturday like clockwork since.

Samson, a nineteen-year veteran on the force, had been making money off payoffs for the better seventeen years of the nineteen. He started at the 77th and headed a six-man team in the drug and robbery division. Samson's crew was all young and fresh on the job faces that were from the hood and taking kickbacks from Butter and Spyda's crew. Internal Affairs could never get anything on them and now the feds was investigating. Samson had a close friend at the bureau who kept him and his crew one step ahead of the investigation, though.

Samson turned over and looked at the clock. "Damn! Three o'clock!" Samson sat up and nudged Jenny. "Yo, it's time for you to go." He then got out of bed and went into the bathroom; he had to be at work by 5 a.m. By the time he exited the bathroom, Jenny was already dressed. Reaching into his wallet, he handed Jenny two hundred dollars, which she accepted before leaving.

Samson dressed and walked into the living room where he had left a plate of cocaine on the coffee table. Picking up the cut-off straw which was lying in the cocaine, he sniffed the powder.

"Yeah! That's what I call a quick pick me up. Now I'm ready to go get the bad guys." Samson smiled at the thought of collecting money from a local drug dealer who was up and coming. Samson picked up the receiver and dialed the cell phone number he took out of his pocket.

"Hello," the voice answered on the other end.

"Yo, Capone, you ready to see me this morning?"

"Damn, Samson, it's three-thirty in the morning."

"That's right; the early bird gets the worm. I'll see you in about a half. Have that for me."

"Yeah, you know where to meet me."

"I'll be there. Oh yeah, Capone, bring some of that good shit you hustle."

"A'ight."

CLICK...

After hanging up, Samson returned to the bedroom to finish dressing.

Samson had joined the force fresh out of high school. At twenty-three, he made detective and for the nineteen years on the force, seventeen of those years he had been on the take, from which he made a good living. He was once married, but due to his lifestyle, his wife of ten years took their two children and moved to the west coast.

RING...RING...RING...

Samson exited his bedroom fully dressed and snatched the cordless phone from off its base. "Yo, talk to me."

"Samson?"

Samson immediately recognized the voice. "If it ain't my favorite FBI man, Agent Smith. What's good? What do you have for your friend today?"

"One of your boys is turning and your crew was mentioned."

"Who?"

"Spyda."

"Damn that bitch nigga! I should've taken that hit on that nigga when Butter offered, but he was paying me good and I didn't wanna lose his money. Damn!"

"It's not too late. They're transporting him to the U.S. Attorney's office at five this morning."

"Are you one of the transporting agents?"

"No."

"Are they friends of yours?"

"If they were, would I call you?"

"Yeah."

"Well, why you ask?"

"Yo, Smith, thanks. Once again, you came to my rescue. I owe you. I got it from here."

"You know where to send the check."

CLICK...

Samson immediately called Bookman and told him to get the boys together. After hanging up with Bookman, he called Capone back and told him that he was leaving the house.

* * * * *

Dice pulled behind a parked van on the corner of Justin's block. They watched Justin stagger into his house and close the door behind him.

"We're going to give it about twenty minutes before you go in. Give him enough time to fall off to sleep." Dice looked at Passion and wondered how good that young pussy was. "Passion...remember, once you go in there, there's no turning back. Once you hit him, get the fuck out of there fast. Make sure you drop the gun in the house. That's why you're wearing the gloves. With no fingerprints, the gun can't be traced back to us." Dice glanced at the clock. "You ready?"

"Yeah."

"Just remember to drop the gun." As Passion got out of the car, Dice noticed a girl entering Justin's house. "Passion, hold up. Get back in the car."

"What?"

"A girl just went into the house."

"I can kill 'em both, then," Passion said with excitement.

"Nah, come on, let's go. We'll get him another time."

Following Dice's orders, Passion got back in the car and they pulled off.

* * * * *

When Penny pulled up in front of her house, she noticed her porch light on.

Somebody must have just left from my door, Penny thought as she exited the car. As she reached the door, she went into her bag and pulled out her keys. As soon as she put the key in the lock, she felt a cold, hard object pressed up against the lower part of her back.

"Don't move or scream, bitch! Just open the door and get in the house," a heavy, baritone voice ordered.

Penny froze with fright. The voice sounded familiar, but she knew better than to turn around as she was shoved into the house. She fell to the floor as the person entered the house and closed the door. Penny expected the worst and prepared herself.

"Bitch, your man Bill Blast is telling, and we have a message for him."

BLOU! BLOU!

Tec fled from the house.

*　*　*　*　*

"Capone, what time are you picking me up in the morning?" Cookie asked as he pulled in front of Summer's house.

"I have something to do first thing in the morning, so I'll be here to pick you up at noon."

"Alright, daddy." Cookie leaned over and gave Capone a kiss.

He smiled at his thoughts and pulled off quickly. Twenty minutes later, Capone was pulling up to Penny's house. Capone reached in his glove compartment and pulled out a couple of condoms. "I'ma fuck the shit out of this pussy!"

When he reached Penny's door, he noticed it was ajar, so he entered. "Yo, Penny!" Capone called out as he walked in. The room was bathed in total darkness. Feeling for the light on the wall, he switched it on. "Oh shit! What the fuck?" Capone ran to check to see if Penny was still alive. As he bent down, he noticed two holes in the back of her head; she had been killed execution style. By the size of the holes, Capone knew a small caliber gun had been used. Without touching anything, Capone hurried and left.

206

* * * * *

As soon as Justin opened the door and saw Summer, it was as if he became sober. Without saying a word, he grabbed her and started kissing on her. The whole time he expressed how sorry he was and how he didn't want to lose her because of the evils of his brothers. Justin promised he would do everything in his power to make whoever was responsible for her sister and grandmother's death pay.

Summer could tell he was drunk; she could smell the liquor on him. Still, she allowed him to lead her to the bedroom where they made love. An hour later, just as Summer expected, Justin was out cold. She got out of his bed, went into his drawer, and took a box of his 9mm bullets. She then took his car keys off the dresser, left the room quietly, and headed out the door. It was time for Cookie to pay for her betrayal.

* * * * *

Dice dropped Passion off at Butter's house, but didn't get out the car. He told her that he had to make a run to the Pj's and to tell Butter that he would call him later. After Passion closed the door behind her and went into Butter's building, Dice pulled off.

Needing to fill up his gas tank, Dice pulled into the gas station on Atlantic and Troy, a block away from the projects. As he got out the car, crackhead Elian ran up to him. "Yo, Dice!"

Aw shit, here comes this begging bitch, Dice thought to himself.

"Yo, Dice, you have something on you?"

"Nah…why you didn't go to the spot?" Dice asked as he pumped the gas.

"You don't know?"

"Come on, Elian, I don't have time for your games. Know what?"

"The feds is running up in the building as we speak. They locked your whole crew up."

"What? Get the fuck out of here!"

"Nah, they're over there right now. I thought you knew. I was going to the spot in Weeksville to cop."

Dice paid the gas attendant and jumped back in his car. He sat there trying to call Butter, but kept getting a busy signal. As he tried dialing the number again, he felt somebody standing over him. Thinking it was crackhead Elian again, he said, "What the fuck you wan-- "

Dice's words were cut short when he looked up and saw Dollar Bill standing over him with a big .40 caliber pointed in his face. Before Dice could react, Dollar Bill pulled the trigger.

* * * * *

Ring...Ring...Ring...

Detective Diekman lay on his bed staring at the ceiling, his mind on Summer. At this moment, he was stuck between a rock and a hard place. He had done his best to remain an honest and trustworthy police officer throughout the years. Diekman had joined the force to make a difference. He had a genuine hate for what his family had done over the years, but the money and temptation had got the best of him. What nobody knew was that Diekman was on the take, as well. However, he made it his business to keep all his dirt as quiet as possible.

Ring...Ring...Ring...

Diekman's thoughts were interrupted by the constant ringing of his phone. As he snatched the receiver up, the base crashed to the floor.

"FUCK!" he screamed as the phone struck his foot. "Son of a bitch! Who the fuck is this?"

"Officer of the law, is that how you answer your phone? I know your mother taught you better manners than that."

Immediately, Diekman recognized the voice. "How many times have I told you not to call me on my home phone?"

"Yeah, yeah, yeah. I know, but this is important. I just got off the phone with our favorite FBI man and he informed me of something that needs to be taken care of...that certain thing you should have already taken care of."

"I'm listening," Diekman said as he peeked out of his living room window.

"Does the name Spyda ring a bell? He's talking and our people want him quiet, and this came down from Russia."

Diekman knew exactly who Samson was talking about and felt somewhat trapped. Once you had any type of dealing with these types of people, you were obligated to them for life. It didn't matter whether you were the police, feds, or whoever. If they did you a favor, they were looking for a long-term relationship.

Trying not to do too much speaking on the phone, Diekman quickly cut Samson off. "Man, it's too much being associated with you."

"That's how you talk to your partner in crime?"

"That's the problem; we're police officers." Diekman felt himself getting frustrated; he knew the feds could be listening in on their conversation because of the investigation of his brother and the police corruption.

"Okay, Officer Diekman, I hear you. But have you spoken to our boys, though?"

"No! And I'll appreciate if you don't call here any more."

CLICK...

Diekman was annoyed by the call; he had told Samson to never contact him at his home. He knew shit was about to get carried away, and if push came to shove, he refused to get caught up in Samson's shit because of his carelessness. The money was good, but to Diekman, his reputation as a good cop meant more. As far as everybody knew he was a good cop, and that was how he wanted to keep it.

Chapter 17
Echoes Or Dreams

Summer walked into the house. All the lights were out, and only an illumination from the TV came from Destiny's room. Summer knew Cookie was home because before she left, she made sure everything was shut off.

This bitch has a lot of nerve sleeping in my sister's bed after what she did, Summer thought to herself as she walked towards the room. She could feel the hatred building up with each step closer she got to the room. *I allowed this bitch to stay in my sister's room, sleep in her bed, and wear her clothes. I should shoot this bitch in the head right in Destiny's bed.* Summer knew she couldn't follow her heart; she would have to take Cookie someplace where the murder could never get traced back to her.

Summer stopped as she stood in the doorway of Destiny's room. She couldn't believe she was about to kill her best friend. Summer entered the room where Cookie laid across the bed fully dressed, with the TV on and cell phone laying by her head on the pillow. Summer started feeling queasy as her stomach knotted up. This was different from the last two people she had killed; this was her best friend. Whatever she was going to do, though, had to be done quickly so she could get back to Justin before he realized she was gone. Summer took a deep breath, exhaled as she walked over to Cookie, and then shook her to awaken her. "Cookie."

Cookie turned over, still half asleep, and looked at Summer with a distorted stare in her half-shut eyes. "Summer! What's wrong?"

"Cookie, get up; I need you to come with me. I have something to show you," Summer said as she turned the lamp on, hoping the light would fully waken her.

"Can't it wait until the morning?" Cookie answered as she tried to turn away from Summer and go back to sleep.

Summer shook Cookie harder as she started getting upset. Summer knew she was pressed for time. "Cookie, come on, get up. I need you to come with me. Come on!" Summer pulled Cookie's feet off of the bed.

"A'ight, I'm up."

"Come on, hurry up. We don't have much time."

"Summer, what the hell is the big rush? What's going on?" Cookie yawned and stretched as she stood up and looked for her sneakers.

"I have something to show you, but we have to leave now."

After Cookie put on her shoes, they hurried out of the house. As Summer approached Justin's car, Cookie stopped and looked at her.

"Girl, whose car do you have?"

"It's Justin Diekman's car," Summer replied while quickly turning her head.

"I thought you told him that you didn't wanna see him no more."

"I did, but I then realized I need him to help me find out who killed my sister."

"True."

Summer pulled off after they were both in the car.

* * * * *

After Samson hung up with Capone, he got in touch with his crew of renegade police and told them about the events surrounding Spyda and what Agent Bookman had told him. He ordered them all to be at the jailhouse in the next twenty minutes.

As Samson rushed through the quite a.m. streets of Brooklyn, headed for the jail where Spyda was being held, his phone started ringing.

"Samson, Penny is dead."

"What?"

"I just left her house; somebody killed her."

"Yo, Capone, don't even sweat that. We was going to have to kill her anyway. She knew too much."

"I don't understand?! Why did you have me tell her to make up that story about Cookie if you was going to kill her anyway?"

"A diversion...all of these people was just pawns in our chess game. They were a stepping stool to the greater picture. Don't worry...with the money we stand to make off of this, you can buy plenty more of them bitches."

"Yeah, I feel you, but what about Cookie?"

"She got to worry about that crazy psycho bitch friend of hers, not us. Listen, Capone, I really don't have time to go through this shit with you right now. I'm on my way to take care of that snitch bitch boy of yours, Spyda. You will see it on the morning news. As far as Penny and your girl Cookie go, chalk them up as casualties of 'Da Game'. You can always get another piece of ass. Whoever killed Penny saved us the time and bullets. If it wasn't for you and that bitch, we wouldn't have to go through all this shit. Rashawn was a good kid, but he was slipping. He cost us twenty million in diamonds because he preferred being with that young piece of pussy instead of being where he was suppose to be. Twenty million in raw fucking diamonds! Capone, you must not realize the pedigree of the people who we're working for. They were pissed off, and the only way I could make any amends was to bring the heads of those responsible for the fuck up, especially that lil' bitch. That tight pussy was the cause for our lil' man slipping. Now we have another chance to get back in with them and maybe get a part of the twenty million. In order for us to do this, we must cover the loose ends. Capone, I'm getting close to my destination. I'll call you later. Remember, look for the breaking news on what happens to your man Spyda."

CLICK...

* * * * *

Summer pulled off the Van Wyck Expressway, and ten minutes later, pulled into a secluded area of Queens behind the Aqueduct Racetrack. "Come on." Summer exited the car and started jogging into the high grass and open fields.

"Summer! Hold the fuck up, girl. You know I'm not with all this running shit. What the hell are we doing out here?" Cookie asked as she struggled to keep up.

"Just come on, Cookie. You will soon see."

As Summer jogged ahead of Cookie, she constantly grabbed at her waistband to prevent the gun from slipping out. There was no turning back now; Cookie had to answer for her betrayal. *It's now or never! This has to be done,* Summer hyped herself up. She stopped, pulling out the gun she had taken from Justice. She could hear Cookie breathing hard as she got closer.

"Damn! I have to stop smoking." Cookie leaned over, trying to catch her breath and breathing hard. "Bitch, would you tell me why the fuck you have me out here on some nature and health shit."

"You don't know?" Summer asked in a low, seductive voice as she kept her back to her.

"Hell no! What the hell is going on?" Cookie straightened up and started walking towards where Summer stood.

As soon as Cookie got within arm's reach, Summer spun. Cookie's puzzled look quickly turned to fear as the glare from the early morning sun reflected off the chrome 9mm Summer held tightly clutched in her hands.

"Cookie, why?"

"Summer, what the hell are you doing? What are you talking about?"

"Cookie, what did my sister and grandmother do to deserve what happened to them? Penny told me it was you. Why?" Summer cocked the 9mm back and pointed it at Cookie.

"Summer, what are you talking about? I didn't have nothing to do with that shit. I don't know what the hell Penny is talking about. She's bugging out." Cookie looked into Summer's eyes and saw no emotions; it was as if Summer wasn't there mentally. The realization hit Cookie that, for some reason, Penny was trying to set her up, but why she had no idea. Cookie raised her hands, as if she could stop the bullets from hitting her.

"Summer, please wait. I have no idea what's going on. You know I wouldn't do anything to hurt you, Destiny, or Ms. Hardy. I don't know why Penny told you that." When Cookie saw that her plea was falling on deaf ears, she attempted to run.

BUNG...BUNG...BUNG...BUNG!!!

Cookie didn't make it but two feet away before being struck in the back with the first shot, which spun her around as she fell in the bushes. Cookie screamed, grunted, and groaned as the pain became unbearable. She prayed Summer wouldn't kill her.

Summer slowly approached. Cookie's mind told her to get up and try to run again, but her body wouldn't respond; she was paralyzed with fear. She looked up with tears in her eyes as the person she would have died for stood over her with the gun pointed directly at her.

"Now it's time for you to pay. And if Penny lied to me...believe me, she will die, as well. I'll see you in my DISTANT ECHOES!"

Summer aimed the gun at Cookie's heart and pulled the trigger.

* * * * *

At exactly 3:45 a.m., the C.O. unlocked Spyda's cell door. "Get dressed. The marshals are coming to get you."

Spyda sat up in his bed. "A'ight."

He knew they were coming to get him so he could meet with the U.S. Attorney, and he would let them know everything regarding who murdered Rashawn, Destiny, and Ms. Hardy. He planned on giving up the police who were behind it all, and telling about the diamonds heist that was

216

still in the works and the main reason for all the killing. If Rashawn had done what he was supposed to do instead of running around with Destiny, shit would have been smooth. Detective Samson had come to Rashawn, Spyda, and Capone with a deal to stick up some Russians, but Rashawn never showed up that night. He forgot to show because he was with Destiny and the shit that went down with Chuck and Hunt being murdered slipped his mind. As a result, Samson had to call off the deal. With Samson working for some big-time Russian mafia cats from Coney Island, they wanted somebody to bleed for the fuck up, but one thing led to another. They were supposed to only hit Rashawn, but being that Destiny saw Capone's and Penny's faces, she had to die, as well.

"Yo, you ready? They're here for you."

Spyda's thoughts were broken by the C.O. standing at his cell. "Yeah, just let me finish brushing my teeth." Spyda leaned over the sink and rinsed his mouth out as the C.O. left from his cell.

Twenty minutes later, Spyda was shackled and led out through the back of the prison into a van.

* * * * *

Samson called his men and told them to be ready because the agents just pulled out of the jail in a black van with Spyda in it and were headed their way. Samson had his men set up three blocks away from the prison. The plan was to intercept the van before they made it to the FDR and to make sure neither Spyda nor the two agents would ever be able to tell anyone else another word. Samson and his partner Jesse, The Body followed the van in a safe distance.

Jesse, The Body was given that name because of his build and his incredible resemblance to the wrestler.

"Yo, Samson, what's the game plan?"

"We make sure Spyda never reaches the U.S Attorney's office, because if he does, that's our asses. So, we got to do all within our power to stop that van." Samson smiled at his partner as he passed him a bag of that raw shit he got from Capone when he met up with him before picking Jesse up. "Two more blocks until the FDR." Samson sped up so he could catch the van.

* * * * *

As Spyda sat shackled in back of the van, he thought about the move he was making. The U.S. Attorney would have to promise to relocate his whole family because what he was about to do was like issuing a death wish for him and his family. Besides the murders a precinct of corrupt police was involved with, there was also the involvement of Russian Mafia.

Spyda wondered how long it would be before he would be released after supplying the officials with this information. *Hell, they should give me an immediate release plus money paid by the government to live comfortable for life,* Spyda thought silently.

Spyda shifted in his restraints, trying to get as comfortable as he could. Law officials always did their best to make the drive as miserable as they could. He watched the shades of passing buildings as he stared coldly out the rear window of the van.

"How much longer?" he asked the two agents as his stomach started growling.

"Just sit back, buddy, and enjoy the ride," the agent who sat shotgun said, while the agent driving made it his business to hit every bump and manhole he could. "Now what are these two dickhead rookie patrolmen waving us down for?"

The driver brought the van to a halt. As the two patrolmen approached the van, the agent rolled down his window.

"Hey guys, we're FBI agents transporting a prisoner." When the driver reached to show his badge, both patrolmen pulled their guns and aimed at the agents. The agents froze with their hands raised high above their heads.

BUNG...BUNG... BUNG... BUNG...BUNG!!!

Spyda jumped at the sound of shots being fired. He began to panic, automatically knowing it was Samson and his crew. The back door swung open and Spyda's fear became reality as he stared down the barrel of Samson's handgun.

"Samson, please..." Before he could finish, Samson and Jesse both fired nine shots into his body.

"Muthafucka, you know that snitches get stitches!" Samson looked at his partner and then to his other two crew members who were in uniforms. "Let's get out of here."

They all jumped in their cars and left the scene of two murdered agents and one snitch.

* * * * *

After leaving the fields, Summer disposed of the gun at the sanitation dump before leaving Queens, and then headed back to Justin's house. When she walked back in Justin's room, he was still knocked out. Summer stripped down to her natural and climbed in the bed with him.

As she got in bed, she noticed his manhood standing erect in his sleep. Quickly becoming aroused, she moved her face closer to his crotch, engulfed his manhood, and began sucking and stroking his shaft until he started moaning and grunting in his sleep. Before long, Justin woke up.

Summer looked into his eyes. "Daddy, I hope you don't mind, but I wanted to give you a treat. Breakfast in bed is played out, so I thought head in bed was a whole lot better. Do you agree?"

Justin just smiled as he grabbed hold of Summer's head and guided her mouth back to its desired place.

While Summer and Justin fucked, she thought about her friend and guilt started to set in. However, thoughts of her sister and grandmother quickly diminished the guilt. As she laid on her back thinking about the events of the last couple of months and how she lost everybody, Justin did his best to please her. It's not that Justin wasn't a good fuck, but although Summer was there physically, her mind was someplace else.

* * * * *

After Dice dropped Passion back at Butter's house, he left. Butter's front door was open, so Passion entered. "Butter!" she called out as she walked towards the bedroom. The closer she got to the bedroom, the louder the sounds which appeared to be moans became. Her heart skipped a beat at the thought of Butter being with another woman after he filled her head with everything she wanted to hear. *Please, God, don't let him be in here with another woman. Let it just be a porno flick he's watching,* Passion said to herself as she continued to walk towards the room.

220

The closer she got, the more she realized it wasn't a porno tape. She heard Butter making the same sounds he made when they made love earlier. Passion's heart raced as she tiptoed and slowly opened the bedroom door.

"Nooooo!" Passion screamed from the sight of seeing the man she was willing to give her life for laid on the bed with another woman who was riding him. Passion gasped for air from the unbearable pain of seeing him fucking someone else.

Sha, who was straddling Butter's manhood, spun around and jumped off of him when she heard Passion scream. "What the fuck?"

"Bitch, get the fuck out of here and close the fucking door!" Butter screamed at Passion.

"Butter, what are you doing? I thought you no longer fucked with her. I thought it was all about us now." Passion's head started spinning as crazy thoughts ran through her head rapidly and she realized he had lied to her. "Butter, why?"

"Bitch, I said get the fuck out of here. I'll deal with you later." Butter jumped out of the bed and ran over to Passion, pushing her to the floor.

Off reaction and hurt, Passion pulled out the gun Dice had given her to kill Justin with and fired. The deafening sound of the gunshot echoed throughout the house as Sha started screaming.

In shock of being shot by Passion, Butter grunted and moaned as he clutched his stomach and collapsed.

"Nooooo!" Sha screamed as she watched Butter hit the floor.

Passion's mind had gone blank, and she didn't realize what she had done until it was too late. She had shot the only person she cared about and loved. Her desire to live was no more. Passion put the barrel of the gun in her own mouth and pulled the trigger.

Chapter 18
Dreams Are Echoes of Reality

"Rashawn, look out!" Destiny screamed as two people ran from behind the van they were parked in back of. Destiny noticed guns in their hands.

"Get down!" Rashawn pushed Destiny down into the seat as he covered her, using his own body as a shield. Destiny screamed at the sounds of the bullets ripping through the car's armor and shattering the glass. As the shooting continued, she could feel as the bullets riddled Rashawn's body. With each impact, she felt his body jerk. When the shooting stopped, Destiny picked her head up.

"Oh my god!" Destiny exclaimed with shock, fear, and puzzlement in her voice as she stared both of the killers in the face. She couldn't believe her eyes. It was as if she was waiting to wake up from this nightmare, but this wasn't no nightmare...this was real and the people that just killed her boyfriend were close friends.

"No!" Destiny jumped out the car. As she ran, confused and scared, she thought about her sister. Did they do something to Summer was the question on her mind, and were they trying to kill her, as well? If they hadn't run out of bullets, would they have killed her, she wondered. Destiny didn't know whether she should go to the police or act like she didn't see anything. But they looked her right in

the face. Would they let her live knowing she could identify them? Destiny had a lot of thoughts running through her head as she ran home, but she couldn't focus on them because her thoughts were on Summer. They better not have hurt Summer, *Destiny thought to herself.*

When Destiny reached her block, she saw the same two who just killed Rashawn run out of her house, jump into their car, and pull off.

"Please let Grandma and Summer be alright," Destiny said to herself as she hid behind a car. She could feel in her stomach that something wasn't right. As the car drove by, Destiny ran from behind the car and into her house.

"Ma! Summer!" she called out as she entered the house. As soon as she took one step inside, she noticed her grandmother lying in a pool of blood. "Nooooo!" Destiny screamed as the tears automatically started pouring down her face. Destiny ran to her grandmother and scooped her up in her arms, but she was already dead. After pulling herself together, she got up and ran to the phone. As she picked up the receiver from off its base, she froze with fear. Penny and Capone were standing in the doorway with their guns drawn.

"Put the phone down."

Destiny placed the receiver down and slowly backed away. "Penny, what are you doing? Why?" Destiny asked, playing on Penny's conscious. Penny just put her head down, consumed by the guilt she felt as she stood in front of Ms. Hardy's dead body.

Before Penny could say a word, Capone spoke, answering for Penny. "You don't know why, Destiny? Your bitch ass man fucked up. He jeopardized a lot of money because he preferred to be with you instead of being where

224

he was supposed to be. Somebody has to answer for what was wronged. As for you and your grandmother, that's not personal; it's business. You saw our faces."

Knowing she was about to die, she turned to Penny for one more attempt of a plea. "Penny, please...you know I won't say nothing." Once again, Penny put her head down. She couldn't stand to look Destiny in the face knowing what was about to happen.

"Look at it like this...because of you, we don't have to kill your sister," Penny said as she raised her weapon and fired.

*   *   *   *   *

Summer woke from her dream screaming. Justin, who lay next to her, jumped up and reached for his service revolver he kept on the nightstand nearby. "Summer, what's the matter? Is everything alright? What's wrong?" Justin noticed she was crying. "Did you have another one of those dreams about your family?"

Summer turned to Justin with tears in her eyes. "I know who killed Destiny," she said as Justin tried his best to comfort her.

"What?" Justin asked, not able to fully understand Summer because her voice was mumbled.

"I said I know who's responsible for killing my sister and grandmother. I saw the whole thing unfold in my dreams. It was Penny and Capone."

"Penny? Isn't Penny your best friend?"

Summer dropped her head as she thought about what she had did to Cookie, her true best friend, suddenly wondering if she had done the right thing. *Did Penny set it up for me to murder Cookie, and if so, why?* Summer thought to herself.

"Summer!" Justin broke Summer out of her deep thoughts. "Isn't Penny your best friend? How can you say Penny had something to do with the murders just because of a dream?"

"I'm sure of it. I've been having these dreams ever since the murders, and in this latest one all the faces were clear as day. It was as if Destiny wanted me to see who did it. This was my sister's way of letting me know."

"Listen, Summer, I know how you feel, but you can't just go kill somebody because of a dream. Even if it's true, and Capone and Penny had something to do with the murders, you have to let the police do their jobs. Believe me, they will get what's due to them for their acts." Justin placed his arm around Summer's shoulder. "Summer, I promise you, we will get whoever is responsible. I'll step to this Capone cat and he will tell me something. Do you know where he lives?"

"He doesn't live too far from here. My girl Cookie was fucking with him."

"Do you think Cookie had something to do with this, too?"

Summer dropped her head. Just thinking about what she did to Cookie and there being a possibility she didn't have nothing to do with it made Summer's stomach turn.

"I hope not," Summer answered in a low whisper. "I feel sick to my stomach." Summer jumped up and ran into the bathroom to throw up. Justin followed closely behind her.

"Are you alright?" Justin asked as he went into the linen closet and got her a washcloth and towel. "There's an extra toothbrush in the medicine cabinet." Justin placed the washcloth and towel on the sink next to where she was bent over the toilet.

"Thank you...I'm alright. All this is just making me sick to my stomach, and I don't think I'ma get better until I get all of those involved." Summer placed her head in the toilet as she felt her last meal coming back up.

Giving her some privacy, Justin went into the living room and turned the TV on to the morning news. A female news reporter stood in front of the entrance of the FDR drive with breaking news. Justin picked up his remote and turned the volume up.

"This has been a morning of blood shed. Two agents and renowned drug dealer Spyda were gunned down early this morning before they got on the FDR headed to the U.S. Attorney's office where Spyda was expected to cooperate and provide names of those involved in several murders and the names of some corrupt cops in return for a lesser sentence. Spyda was recently arrested on charges of gun possession, conspiracy to distribute crack cocaine, and conspiracy to commit murder. At this moment, the police have no suspects and there's no further information. We will keep you posted as we learn more about this breaking case.

"In other news, a sixteen-year-old girl who finds her boyfriend, who is ten years her senior, in bed with another woman, shoots the boyfriend and then turns the gun on herself. The boyfriend is a known drug dealer and the leader of the notorious Blood gang in the Brooklyn section of New York. Michael Diekman a.k.a. Butter Bean is also the brother of Detective Justin Diekman. Michael was shot in the stomach and is expected to make a full recovery. As for the girl, whose name will not be disclosed because of her age, she was pronounced dead at the scene.

"Our final story, police responded to a call of shots fired at 316 Dekalb Street and found Penny Black shot to death in her home. Police have no leads and are asking for information involving the death."

Upon walking in and catching the last of the news, Summer recognized the house and immediately knew it was Penny's house. "Justin, that's Penny's house!" she said while pointing at the TV.

Then it hit Justin why the name sounded so familiar. Justin turned to Summer with a concerned look. "Do you think all the killings are related? Somebody probably killed her to hush her up, plus the agents and Spyda being killed, not to mention my brother being shot last night."

"What? Your brother was killed last night?"

"No, he was shot, but he'll live. The news reporter said he was shot because his girl caught him in bed with another woman, but I don't believe that. Whatever he got, believe me, he deserves it." Justin looked at his arm cast. "I think we should step to Capone tonight before he comes up dead, as well. Have you spoken to your friend Cookie?"

"No, not since yesterday."

"I'm going to make a few calls and see what I can come up with."

"Justin, fuck going to the police. These people murdered my family, and their fate should be the same. Jail is too good for them; anyway, the police might be involved." Summer returned to the bathroom and ran water for her shower. Justin stood in the doorway of the bathroom and watched as she undressed, then walked up behind her and started caressing her from behind.

"Summer, please, trust me. I'm not going to let you or your family down. Please, believe me. Whoever is responsible will pay with the most severe punishment. This I put on my life."

Justine started kissing and sucking on Summer's neck while rubbing on her breast. Then, he leaned Summer forward, bending her over the sink, while he got on his knees and started eating her out from the back.

*   *   *   *   *

Samson pulled up to Marco's, one of the hottest Russian nightclubs in Coney Island, Brooklyn. Over a hundred partygoers were waiting outside to get in the club. The majority of the partygoers were young Russian women. All you saw was blonde hair and boob, ass, and lip jobs. Three huge Russian bouncers guarded the door behind the velvet rope, carefully choosing who entered and who didn't. On nights like this, they could easily make anywhere from fifteen hundred to two thousand dollars on the side just from people who wanted to get in the club that bad but who didn't have any clout. This was the place to be if you were young and Russian, and they would pay good money to rub elbows with the club's VIP A-List.

Samson approached the bouncers, who he knew from numerous encounters. The bouncers were also soldiers in the Russian Mafia. The bouncer gave Samson a nod, which meant it was okay for one to enter the club and party amongst the elite of partygoers made up of mostly Russian mobsters, entertainers, and other people who had some type of clout in the Russian community. Samson returned the head nod as he walked by the head bouncer and entered the club. The club, which was already filled to capacity, pumped not Russian music, but rap music. The latest release from 50 Cent blared from the speakers as

Samson maneuvered through the packed dance floor and headed for Ivan's reserved booth in the VIP section.

Ivan Krusovh, a short, dark complexion, husky Russian with short, black, stringy hair and slightly balding in the middle, was one of the top lieutenants in the Russian mob and Samson's connect. Samson never dealt directly with the bosses, only through Ivan.

Ivan sat at his booth with a blonde-haired girl with the biggest tit job in the joint; the girl couldn't have been more than seventeen or eighteen years old. Ivan had his face leaned over in a plate of cocaine he had in front of him. The blonde patiently waited for her turn of the get high. When Samson approached the booth, Ivan raised his head from the plate. That's when Samson noticed there was a second woman whose head was between Ivan's lap giving him head while he snorted the cocaine. The girl raised her head when she heard Samson approach.

"Damn, Ivan baby, you Russians sure know how to do it big. Y'all know how to get the party started right," Samson said as he smiled at both girls.

"Samson, my favorite corrupt detective. Here, have a seat." Ivan motioned for the girl who just raised her head from his lap to get up and let Samson slide in. "You like?" Ivan asked as he pushed the plate of cocaine towards him.

"That's what I'm talking about! Don't mind if I do." Samson took a seat, picked the cut-off straw up from the plate, and started doing lines.

Ivan once again motioned for the girl to take care of Samson, and before Samson could react, the girl was unzipping his pants, pulling out his manhood, and putting his cock into her mouth.

"Wow!" Samson paused for a moment to gain his composure as the feeling of the girl's hot, wet mouth sent chills through his body. "This right here is the fucking life. There's nothing more pleasurable than sniffing cocaine and getting your head sucked. This is why I love you fucking Russians."

Samson paused as he felt the girl's tongue twirl around the shaft of his cock. Closing his eyes, he tried his best not to moan. Unable to hold back the shivers that shot through his whole body, he started cumming. The girl continued to work his manhood as he filled her jaws with his hot semen. Samson gripped the edge of the table and tried his best not to make a noise, already embarrassed he was cumming so soon. He looked at Ivan and the other girl who were both smiling. The girl lifted her head from Samson's lap and licked her lips.

"All done, daddy," she said to Ivan, letting him know she did what he ordered.

"Damn! She's good!" Samson said as he fixed his pants and continued to do a couple more lines of coke.

"Damn, Samson, you finish so fast, no!" Ivan said as him and the other girl laughed. Samson pushed the plate to the girl who had just finished pleasing him. To him, she deserved it. "So, Samson, did you enjoy Eva's talent?"

"Boy, did I? Can I take her home with me?"

"Sure, you can. You can have any of these women here if your money is long enough." Ivan motioned for the girls to give him and Samson a little privacy for a minute while they talked. Both girls got up and went to the ladies room.

"Samson, the boss wants to know if you took care of that little situation."

"Tell them old gangsters that everything is clear. Spyda never made it to his destination, plus he has two less agents to worry about."

"Good, because a lot of people was getting nervous. Besides that, we have somebody that stole some money and went into hiding. Of course, we found out where he is hiding. So, I need you to go take care of that for us at once."

Chapter 19
Murder Was The Case

Butter laid in his hospital bed with his mind on Passion. Her suicide crushed him. Although she had shot him, Butter still had feelings for her.

During Sha's visit, she informed him about Dice being murdered and nobody knowing who did it. The war was finally over. Spyda was murdered and the majority of his crew was dead or in jail. The only ones Butter still had out there was Two-Guns Paul and the twins; the rest of his crew was locked up, and he just got word that Gutter was cooperating with the feds, so he knew it was only a matter of time before they would come for him. Butter never found out if Dice and Passion ever took care of the situation with his brother. That was another issue weighing heavily on his mind.

Butter had lost a lot of blood from the gunshot wound to his stomach, and he was still pretty weak, but he knew he had to hurry and get out of there. He knew it was only a matter of time before the feds came running through the doors to lock him up for some shit with this war. There were too many running their mouths, and with Gutter telling, he was as good as told on. Butter knew Half Pint would hold his head because he was from the old school, but Gutter was broke from a different cloth; he was from upstate and his loyalty wasn't as strong as the rest of them because when all is said and done, his home is not Brooklyn. And you know what they say, 'Your home is where the heart is.'

As Butter lay in the bed, he thought about the war with Spyda and how it wasn't even worth it because in the long run nothing was gained except the loss of life, friends, and being on the run. Hearing a slight knock, Butter quickly turned his head to his room door. He hoped it was Two-Guns Paul because he had told Sha to make sure Two-Guns came to get him. As the door opened, Butter stared into the eyes of his brother Justin with hatred.

Justin entered with a smirk on his face as he walked over to the bed. "What's up, brotha? I see you got yourself in a jam. I feel bad for the young lady. I hate to see a life go to waste over somebody like you, who don't give a fuck about nothing but himself. I know you must be real proud of yourself, having women wanting to kill themselves over you."

If Butter had the strength, he would have rushed him, but he had to save his little strength for when Two-Guns got there so he could leave.

Butter spoke in a low whisper, "What the fuck do you want?"

"Listen, you are my brother; we come from the same wound. I'm not here to fight with you. You have a lot on your hands. I'm actually here for your assistance. I need you to help me with the murders of Destiny and her grandmother. I know you didn't have anything to do with them, but I also know you know something. Butter, I need your help, and then you will never have to worry about me again. Your whole crew is either dead or in jail, and the same with Spyda's crew. When does all this foolishness end?"

"This will never end. As long as you're still alive, this shit will never end. You will be my enemy for the rest of our lives. I will never help you or any other police, feds, or D.A. with shit. So do your own job. Me helping the pigs with anything will never happen."

"Is this how you want it to be, my brother? This is not about me and you. It's about the senseless murder of a sixteen-year-old and her grandmother."

"Don't address me as any kin of yours; you are dead to me. I'm tired, so I would appreciate it if you would do me a favor and get the fuck out of my room." Butter turned his head away from Justin.

"Okay, but I'll always be your brother, and remember, this is not about you and me." Justin turned to leave the room. As he walked towards the elevator, he noticed the feds entering Butter's room. Justin just smiled as he entered the elevator.

*   *   *   *   *

When Two-Guns Paul entered the hospital, he noticed the feds escorting a handcuffed Butter off of the elevator in a wheelchair. Two-Guns quickly ducked into the hospital's cafeteria, watching as they left out the hospital, placed Butter into their van, and pulled off.

Damn, Two-Guns thought as he left the hospital in a hurry. He knew he would have to get out of town, because if they got Butter, he knew he would be next. He called the twins and told them to collect whatever they had in the streets from whoever was still out there.

That night, Two-Guns Paul crept to the Pj's to collect everything so he and the twins could jet down south until shit cooled off. The twins had family in Virginia that they were gonna stay with for a while and set up shop. Beside the runners and a couple of the no-name soldiers, the whole crew got snatched up in the raid. The Pj's looked like a ghost town.

"Yo, Lil' Paul!" a voice called out from behind as Two-Guns stepped out of his car.

Who the fuck is calling me Lil' Paul? Two-Guns thought as he turned around. The only people who called him Lil' Paul were the people who knew his father. Two-Guns was named Paul after his father, who was one of the most respected gangsters in the Pj's back in the days. Big Paul had been murdered in prison. Some say he was murdered over a Gump; others say the C.O.'s put a hit out on him because he was fucking the captain's wife who was also a C.O. at the prison.

When Two-Guns turned around, Dollar Bill was walking towards him. Dollar Bill worked for Two-Gun's father and was said to be the reason his parents broke up, because Dollar Bill was fucking his mother and his father found out when he went to prison. Dollar Bill was from the old side, but in those days, the Pj's wasn't separated like it was today. Two-Guns hadn't seen Dollar Bill in years.

"Yo, Dollar Bill! What's up, old timer? When you get out?"

Without answering, Dollar Bill pulled out his piece. Two-Guns froze before reacting, but it was too late.

BUNG...BUNG...BUNG!!!

Two-Guns dropped to the ground as Dollar Bill ran and stood over top of him. "Tell your punk ass father that I'll see him in hell. The first bullets were what I owed your father."

Bung!!!

"That one's from Spyda." Dollar Bill ran off.

* * * * *

Summer sat on Justin's couch as the TV watched her; she was in deep thought. The last four months had been a living hell. She thought about her friends Cookie and Penny, who were now both dead. Summer was really all alone now and what made it worst was that she was now a stone cold killer, an animal like the people who killed her sister and grandmother. Summer had murdered three people in a matter of days, one of whom was her best friend, and now she believed Penny, her other best friend, was responsible for the murders of her family because of a dream. To Summer, her dreams were how her sister communicated with her, but she would never found out if this was true or not because Penny was murdered last night.

Who killed Penny and why? Was this connected to the murders? Summer asked herself as her thoughts were interrupted by Justin's phone ringing. Startled, she jumped, and then slowly got up off the couch and answered it.

"Hello."

"Summer, it's me. I just left Penny's house, and I found something I think you should see. I'm on my way."

"Do the police know who killed her or why?'

"No, but whoever killed her was involved with the murders of your family. I'm on my way. Stay put, I'll be there in about a half."

Hanging up the phone, Summer wondered what Justin had found at Penny's house. *Did he find the gun used in the murder? Was Penny really the one who killed my family and just used Cookie as an escape goat?* Whatever it was, Justin would be there soon and her questions would be answered. *Please, God, I hope I didn't murder my best friend for no reason,* Summer thought as she sat back on the couch and waited for Justin to return home.

About twenty minutes later, Justin entered the house carrying in his hand what appeared to be a book of some sort. He walked up to Summer and handed it to her. It was Penny's diary.

"Summer, I hate to say it, but your friend was involved with the murders. June nineteenth was the date of the murders; turn to the page dated June nineteenth." Justin sat down next to Summer and waited for her to read.

Summer looked at Justin with a somber expression and then opened the diary.

> *6/19*
>
> *Dear Diary,*
>
> *Today I have participated in something that turned out to be the worst thing in my life, something that went totally wrong and I don't know how I'm going to live with myself. I killed my best friend's sister and her grandmother. It wasn't supposed to happen like that. We was only supposed to kill Rashawn, but Destiny saw our faces, so Capone forced me to kill her. I didn't want to, but I knew I had to or the people who we was working for would have killed us. I pray that God forgives me. Destiny, I'm so sorry.*
>
> *~Penny*

Summer looked up with tears in her eyes; her dreams were true. Now she knew for certain Destiny was letting her know who killed her, but her tears were because she felt guilty about murdering Cookie. *Did Cookie have anything to do with the murders?* Summer wondered.

"Summer, that's not all. Turn to the page dated September nineteenth, which was yesterday. This is why I had to take this book and couldn't let it get into the hands of the investigating officers."

Summer turned to the page dated September nineteenth and started reading again.

9/19
Dear Diary,
I hate myself even more today. I don't know how much more of this I can take. How long does this have to go on before it's over? I feel that my life is in danger. I'm pregnant and I don't know who the father of my child is. I've been sleeping with my cousin's man, Capone, and Bill Blast at the same time. I have been sleeping with her man behind her back ever since they've been together. And today, at the request of Capone, I told Summer that Cookie was involved in the killing of her family in order to take the tension off of me. Capone knew Summer would kill Cookie. Summer had already killed Lil' Justice and Beast. She swore to kill everybody that was rumored to have anything to do with the murders. And as I write this, Cookie is probably already dead. Each day I hate myself more. Cookie, I pray you can forgive me for my betrayal.
~Penny

As Summer closed the diary, she could feel Justin staring at her, waiting for an answer. She picked her head up and looked at Justin with tears in her eyes. Cookie was innocent and she had murdered her.

"Summer, they found Cookie's body in the fields behind the Aqueduct Racetrack in Queens tonight. Don't say nothing. Nobody saw this book. I found it before any of the investigating officers saw it."

Once again, Summer remained quiet and dropped her head. She was heartbroken and destroyed. She had killed her only friend and was betrayed by the other one. The man who was the brother of the killers of her parents was all she had, and he knew what she had done. Justin sat down beside Summer and placed his arm around her.

"Summer, listen, I don't wanna know whether you did this or not. I love you, and I'm willing to spend the rest of my life with you. But please, let me help you. You are not alone. As for what's in this here diary, this information can send you away for the rest of your life. But as of now, it served its purpose. We know who's responsible." Justin then stood up, walked over to the front door, opened it, and placed the diary on the ground in his front yard, lighting a match to it.

"Summer!" he called out to her as he set the book on fire. "What's in this book is between you and me and to never be spoken about again." Justin watched as the diary burned to ashes. When the diary finished burning, Justin walked back into the house and sat down on the couch next to Summer. "Now we have to go see Capone because he can tie you in with the murder of Cookie. He can also tell us who they were working for and who gave the order to murder Rashawn, Destiny, and your grandmother. Summer, I'm with you, and I promise you every person involved will pay. Capone must die, but I don't want you going after him. Let me handle him. I am the police; I'm licensed to kill the bad guys. So promise me that you will let me handle this from here on."

Summer shook her head in agreement as Justin picked her up and carried her into the bedroom.

Chapter 20
To Catch A Murderer

A week had passed since the murder of Spyda and Butter's arrest. The Pj's was scared and new; younger faces were out in front of the buildings trying to get their hustle on with the absence of the two crews. Dollar Bill had the entire Pj's on lock and was copping weight from Capone. Dollar Bill was back on top and Capone was the man. Capone got his weight from Samson, who was supplied by the Russians. Now it was time for Capone to handle the councilman situation.

For it to be a Saturday night, everything was at a scary silence. The streets were a ghost town as Capone and Sha drove towards their destination. You could feel the tension in the air. Whenever shit was too calm in New York, you knew it was the quiet before the storm. Capone didn't agree with the job Samson gave him. To kill a councilman was big…equal to killing a police officer. However, Capone knew he couldn't refuse the job. Shit had got out of hand and Capone was starting to get nervous. With Cookie and Penny both dead, Capone wondered if he was next. *Who killed Penny if it wasn't Samson and his crew of police,* Capone asked himself. Fearing for his life, he decided that after this job he would take Isis, his son, and get out of town.

"Capone, you alright?" Sha asked as she noticed her brother's mind being elsewhere.

"Yeah, sis, shit is just getting crazy. You know they found Cookie dead and Penny murdered."

"Wasn't it the plan to have Cookie killed?"

"Yeah, but who murdered Penny? Samson said it wasn't him. This shit got me a lil' shook."

"Don't worry, big bro, I got your back," Sha said as she checked her gun to make sure she had a full clip, just in case shit got out of hand with the councilman.

Capone decided to take his sister with him; they could live good and comfortable off of the money they could make off this job. Samson told Capone it was anywhere from one to two million in cash in the councilman's safe. After the money was taken, twenty-five percent would be given to the bosses, another twenty-five percent would be given to Samson, and the remainder would be for Capone and Sha. Of course, Capone would never tell Samson how much they actually took from the councilman's house. But if it was the amount of money Samson told him, they stood to make at least a quarter million for themselves.

As Capone entered the block filled with million dollar homes, he turned the headlights off. This was the only section in Brooklyn that had houses worth this amount of money. The houses in this section were historical and all worth money.

"Yo, sis, you ready? That's the house right there." Capone pointed to a two-story brownstone house on the corner with a big yard and porch.

Sha smiled as she shook her head in agreement. "Let's do this. Let's get this money."

242

"Remember, Sha, ring the bell and as soon as he answers the door, you hit him with the game about your car stalling on the corner and having to use his phone to call your mother. As soon as he opens the door to let you in, I'm gonna rush in. I'ma be on the side of the house so he can't see me when he comes to the door. You hold him at gunpoint while I make sure nobody else is in the house."

"What about wife and kids?"

"The fucker is a Gump. He's gay."

"So...just because he's gay doesn't mean he don't have no wife and kids. Look at the muthafuckin' governor of New Jersey. He had a wife."

"That's why you hold him down while I check the house. He don't have no family, but just in case he has one of his gay lovers up in there with him. Are you ready?"

"Yeah, let's do this."

Capone and Sha both exited the car and walked towards the house quickly. As they walked up onto the porch, Capone stood off to the side so he couldn't be seen while Sha rung the doorbell. Three minutes later, the councilman who was a frail, light skin, black man answered the door wearing his bathrobe.

"Yes, can I help you, young lady?" the councilman asked through his screen door.

"Oh yes, thank you. My car stopped on the corner and I was wondering if I can use your phone to get in touch with my parents. I knocked on three different doors and nobody seems to be home tonight. I'm sorry to bother you, sir, but my cell phone battery is dead and I don't have no change on me to use the pay phone," Sha explained in a polite, innocent, and convincing voice.

"Oh please, of course, come on in." As the councilman opened his screen door to let Sha in, Capone rushed from the side of the house, knocking the councilman down to the ground as him and Sha rushed in.

"Oh my god! Please, what's going on?" the councilman asked as he watched Sha and Capone enter with their guns drawn.

"Muthafucka, you know what this is. Who else is in the house?" Capone demanded as he ran by the councilman, not waiting for his response.

"Please don't kill me. I have money in the safe. I can give you everything. Please, just don't kill me." The councilman pleaded for his life as Capone entered back in the room.

"Who's upstairs? Is anybody else in this house with you?"

"Please, don't kill me!"

CRACK!

"Stop crying, bitch nigga, and answer my question before I kill you right now."

"No, I'm the only one that's here. The housekeeper is off tonight."

"Where's the money?"

"Upstairs in the safe. I'll give it to you. Please, just don't kill me."

"Come on." Capone turned to Sha. "Hold the door down."

"A'ight, just hurry up." Sha walked over and looked out the window as Capone led the councilman up the stairs to his bedroom.

"Please, I have 1.5 million in cash. Y'all can have it; just let me live."

Capone led him to the safe behind a picture on the wall. "If you make the wrong move, I'ma shoot you in the head. So be easy."

The councilman opened the safe, revealing stacks of money. Capone snatched the sheet off the bed. "Put the money in this and wrap it up."

"Please, sir...anything...just don't kill me." The councilman packed the money in the sheet and passed it to Capone.

"Now get on your knees, face the wall, and don't get up until you hear my car pull off."

The councilman quickly did as he was told, thankful that Capone wasn't going to kill him.

As Capone started walking out the room, he turned back around. "Oh yeah, I have a message from the Russians." The councilman quickly turned around, knowing he was going to be killed once he heard the mentioning of the Russians.

"No! Pleeease!" The councilman raised his hand to shield his face, but it was useless. Capone fired two shots to his body, dropping him, and then he walked up to him and put one in his head. Capone turned and ran out the room with the sheet filled with money. As he ran down the stairs, Sha had her weapon pointed at him just in case shit went crazy upstairs and the councilman got the best of Capone.

"Sha, it's me!" Capone screamed as he saw Sha's gun pointed at his head. "Come on, I have the money."

They both ran out the house, jumped in the car, and pulled off.

"Did you get all the money?" Sha asked as she drove away from the house.

"Yeah, we got 1.5, and I'ma tell them that he only had one million. I want you to drop me off at the crib and you take the five hundred thousand and wait for me at the hotel."

"Yes! We came off!" Sha screamed as she headed for Capone's crib.

* * * * *

Around three o'clock that morning, Justin quietly climbed out of bed. Assuming Summer was asleep, he got dressed. Justin constantly looked back to make sure he hadn't awakened Summer. Quietly, he crept out the room, got the keys to his unmarked police car, and pulled off.

Summer was wake the whole time, and as soon as she heard him pull off, she hurried and got dress. Snatching his car keys off the dresser, she ran out the house behind him, following behind at a safe distance.

Justin pulled into a one-way alley surrounded by warehouses. Summer kept driving and parked at the corner, then hurried and ran back to the block. Summer noticed a police officer in uniform and another man with a white bag or what looked like a sheet with something in it. Summer froze when she recognized who the person was. It was Capone, but she didn't recognize the officers. Justin and the two men entered the building. When Summer saw it was clear, she followed. Noticing a window open on the second level of the building, she climbed on top of a garbage can, grabbed hold of the ledge, and pulled herself up and into the window, where she watched what was going on from the ledge.

* * * * *

"Hey, what's good, Justin? I hear they took you off of the case. That's not good." Samson turned on the lights in the office as he held the door open for Justin and Capone.

"Yeah, this shit has gone too far. Have you spoken to Ivan about the diamonds? We're going to have to do this soon because shit is getting too hot." Justin looked at Capone and gave him a head nod.

"What's up, Justin? I heard your brother got knocked," Capone asked.

"Yeah, he was a little too reckless anyway."

"Yeah, I heard he tried to get you whacked the other night." Samson pointed at the cast on Justin's arm.

"Yeah, they tried, but I'm the police. I've been trained for this." Justin smiled as Samson pulled out his bag of cocaine and passed it to Justin.

"Yeah, well, let's see how much money we have."

They both turned to Capone, who placed the sheet on the table and untied it.

"He said he only had one million."

"What? You fucking lying little bitch!" Samson pulled out his 9mm and put it to Capone's head. "Don't fucking lie to me."

"I'm not lying. This was all he had." Capone pleaded.

Justin grabbed Samson. "Calm down." He grabbed Samson's gun and made him lower it. "Take it easy, baby boy. That's a good little hit. After we give the bosses the seven hundred and fifty thousand plus his twenty-five percent, we split 62.5 thousand."

"Justin, I know this lil' shit is holding out on us," Samson said as he placed his gun back into the holster.

"Is that what you think, Samson?" Justin asked.

"I know that gay bastard had about two million in the house tonight. He collected off of them construction contracts big time, and you know he couldn't put the money in no banks. So the bosses said he would have the money in the house. This lil' shit is playing and robbing us."

As soon as Samson finished, Justin pulled out his heat and pointed at Capone's head. He looked Capone in the eyes and pulled the trigger. Then, without warning, he turned and pointed at Samson.

"Justin, what the fuck is you doing?" Samson asked as he looked into Justin's eyes.

"This is not personal; it's just business." After pulling the trigger, Justin started wrapping the money back up in the sheet before hearing a crashing sound out front. He finished wrapping the money in the sheet and ran to the door, but nobody was there.

Justin quickly jumped in the unmarked vehicle and pulled off.

* * * * *

When Justin shot Capone and the police officer, Summer fell from the ledge. She couldn't believe what she had witnessed. Justin was involved with what was going on.

Summer hid behind the garbage as Justin ran out of the warehouse, jumped in the unmarked, and pulled off. She then ran to the car and followed him again. She knew he wasn't going back to the house; he would have to stash the money somewhere else, so she followed him. Justin was somehow involved with everything that had been going on, including the murders of her sister and grandmother. So many questions were running through her head as she followed behind him.

As she drove, she looked in Justin's glove department. "Bingo!" Summer said as she pulled out his .38 service revolver. While steering the car with one hand, she checked to see if the gun was loaded. "Yes!" The gun was fully loaded with six shots...just enough to do what she had to do.

* * * * *

After Capone dropped Sha off at the hotel, she made a phone call and waited for the outcome. As she lay on the bed watching BET, she heard a car door close. Immediately, she rushed and opened the front door, smiling when she saw the face. She jumped in his arms and started tongue kissing him. Justin closed the door behind him as Sha dropped to her knees and unzipped his pants. He dropped the sheet of money on the floor while Sha deep throated his manhood. She didn't even think about what had happened to her brother. They had 1.5 million dollars to split between them. Her brother was just another casualty of 'Da Game'.

"Baby, do you have the other money?" Justin asked as he picked her up and led her to the bed.

"Yes, daddy, right there on the table. We can count it after you take care of this pussy that's been fiending for your touch all night."

Sha pulled Justin on top of her as she started pulling his shirt off. Making his way to her panties, he ripped them off and quickly dived in for a swim. He worked Sha's cunt with his middle and index fingers, rubbing gently and fast. The more Sha moaned the more speed Justin increased with his fingers. Positioning his mouth over her womanhood, he opened his mouth to taste her sweetness. As soon as

Justin's tongue touched her flesh, it sent shocks through her whole body. The sensation of his tongue was magic; he knew exactly how to please a woman with his tongue. The circular motion with the tip of his tongue sent surges of pleasure to her toes as he concentrated on her clit.

BOOM!

The front door of the hotel room flew open. Sha jumped up as Justin quickly turned around. There stood Summer in the doorway, pointing the revolver.

"Summer!" Justin screamed.

"Summer?!" Sha asked to herself, and then fear set in. Sha tried to reach for the gun that was on the nightstand.

POP...POP...POP!!!

Sha dropped.

"Nooooo!" Justin screamed as he started to run for Sha.

"Justin, don't move if you wanna leave here alive," Summer said while aiming at Justin's head.

"Summer, please, let me explain."

"You can't explain anything. Just tell me who you work for? Who's the bosses?"

"Summer, please, wait a minute. This thing is bigger than you. Let me help you. You can't do this by yourself. These people are big; they have a lot of pull."

"Yeah, and your ass is one of them, just like the one you murdered back at the warehouse."

Justin knew Summer would kill him, so he tried to make a move, hoping she wouldn't shoot him. Wrong move.

POP...POP!!!

Justin clutched his stomach as he fell to the ground.

Summer walked over and stood over top of him. "You betrayed me. Your family murdered my family. You turned my best friend against me. Why? What did my family do to you? You at least owe me that much. Tell me, what did my family do to you?"

Justin coughed as blood poured from his mouth. He knew he wouldn't live much longer. He was losing breath, blood was in his lungs, and he knew he would soon suffocate in his own blood. Justin decided to tell Summer what she wanted to know…why her family was doomed to die and by whom.

"Summer," Justin began in a faint voice, "your father stabbed up a Russian real bad when he was in prison. That Russian was the son of Ivan Krusovh, a top man in the Russian mafia. Ivan Krusovh put the hit out on your father that night at the club. He paid my brothers. I didn't know this at the time, and I was the one that turned my brothers in. I didn't have nothing to do with this shit at the time."

Cough! Cough! Justin tried to catch his breath as the struggle to breath was painful. The night your sister and grandmother were murdered it was Penny and Capone. Ivan had put the hit out on Rashawn for messing up a deal worth millions in raw diamonds, and Destiny saw who it was and so she had to be murdered. *Cough! Cough!* "Summer, I'm sorry. Destiny and your grandmother weren't supposed to die."

Summer cried profusely as she raised the gun and pointed it at Justin's head. "This is for my family."

POP!!!

With the last shot in the revolver, Summer finished Justin off. Before fleeing the hotel, she collected the money off the table and in the sheet. .

Epilogue

Six months later…

Summer sat at a table surrounded by young Russian men who were fiending for her attention. Across from her sat Ivan with two big titty, blonde hair young girls indulging in their normal. Ivan was coked out beyond recognition, but today, the girls he had with him worked for somebody else. And the cocaine he was sniffing like it was going out of style wasn't really cocaine, but rat poison mixed with cyanide acid.

Summer watched as Ivan's eyes rolled in the back of his head after sniffing another line of the poison. Ivan's head dropped as the two girls quietly got up and left the table. As they passed Summer, they gave her a slight head nod and a smile to let her know it was done. Summer looked at Ivan slumped over in the plate of poison and smiled as she got up to leave.

"Okay, boys, I have to leave now. It's getting late and my husband will be worried. I enjoyed y'alls company." Summer gave the guys a flirtatious smile and blew them a kiss as she walked out the club

Summer laughed to herself as the feeling of foreclosure set in. She felt somewhat relieved that her sister and grandmother could rest in peace now. As she left the club, Summer could hear the DISTANT ECHOES of her sister's laughter drowning out the music that blared from the club's speakers.

"Yeah, lil sis, y'all can rest in peace, and your cries are no more than DISTANT ECHOES! I love you."

THE END

James I-God Morris